"I Remember Your Passion...."

Valerio's voice was vibrant and Helena could feel the heat of his breath against her shoulder. She turned to stare at him and for a moment he leaned toward her.

Then something happened to him. He stopped abruptly, as though constrained, and she knew he was afraid. He wanted to touch her, wanted it so desperately that he dared not venture even the lightest contact.

Her flesh was burning. Once before, years ago, just being with him had made her feel this way, as if he was passionately kissing her even while he kept his distance. The familiar feelings assailed her again and she was left shaking.

Valerio wanted to reclaim what he still considered his own.

Dear Reader:

SILHOUETTE DESIRE is an exciting new line of contemporary romances from Silhouette Books. During the past year, many Silhouette readers have written in telling us what other types of stories they'd like to read from Silhouette, and we've kept these comments and suggestions in mind in developing SILHOUETTE DESIRE.

DESIREs feature all of the elements you like to see in a romance, plus a more sensual, provocative story. So if you want to experience all the excitement, passion and joy of falling in love, then SILHOUETTE DESIRE is for you.

For more details write to:

Jane Nicholls
Silhouette Books
PO Box 236
Thornton Road
Croydon
Surrey CR9 3RU

LUCY GORDON
A Coldhearted Man

Silhouette Desire

Originally Published by Silhouette Books
division of
Harlequin Enterprises Ltd.

First published in Great Britain 1986
by Silhouette Books, 15–16 Brook's Mews, London W1A 1DR

© Lucy Gordon 1985

Silhouette, Silhouette Desire and Colophon are Trade Marks
of Harlequin Enterprises B.V.

ISBN 0 373 05245 6

22–0486

Made and printed in Great Britain for
Mills & Boon Ltd by
Richard Clay (The Chaucer Press) Ltd,
Bungay, Suffolk

LUCY GORDON
lives in Venice with her Italian husband and three
cats. For twelve years she was a writer on an English
women's magazine but left to be a full-time novelist.
When not writing, she likes to travel extensively and
go to the theatre as much as possible.

Other Silhouette Books by Lucy Gordon

Silhouette Special Edition

Legacy of Fire
Enchantment in Venice

Silhouette Desire

Take All Myself
The Judgement of Paris

For further information about
Silhouette Books please write to:

Jane Nicholls
Silhouette Books
PO Box 236
Thornton Road
Croydon
Surrey CR9 3RU

For Gloria,
without whom this book would never have been written.

Prologue

For God's sake, look out!"

Helena didn't know who shrieked the terrified words. It
might have been she or one of the other two people in the car
with her. She was blinded by the headlamps of the oncoming
truck. There was a moment's panic-stricken confusion over the
car's unfamiliar left-hand steering, then her hands tightened on
the wheel, which seemed to leap sideways.

The car swerved violently and to her horror she saw that it
had turned directly into the path of the truck. She had a moment's blinding vision of the driver, his face ghastly as he
struggled to wrench his wheel aside. Then the world was full of
fearsome noise, the sound of metal being crushed like tissue
paper, smashed glass falling to the road and the demented
screaming that seemed to go on and on and on....

One

The pain in her head was intolerable, and it became worse as soon as she opened her eyes. She was in a room where everything seemed to be white, and the brilliance beat down on her. She raised an arm to shield her eyes and discovered that even this small movement hurt. There was the sound of curtains being drawn across a window, and a quiet voice said, "That's better for you, isn't it?"

She hadn't known there was anyone else in the room, but at the sound she looked sideways and realized that she had two companions. One was a middle-aged woman in a white uniform, whose veil proclaimed her to be a nun. The other was a man in his sixties, who leaned close to her and said abruptly, "Thank God you've come around at last!"

"Have I been out long?" she murmured.

"About thirty-six hours," said the man. "You've come close to surfacing several times, but this is the first time you've made it."

"Don't make her talk too much," said the nun. "It's too soon."

"I realize that," said the man, "but as soon as the police know she's conscious they'll be in here wanting to ask questions." His voice was harsh but it was the harshness of concern. Helena could feel his genuine anxiety, and she tried to force herself to concentrate.

"Police?" she said. "Why? Who are you, where am I?"

"You're in the Heart of Mercy Hospital in Florence. The three of you were brought here after the accident. My name is John Driffield. I work in the British consulate here in Florence. We got a message to say that two Britishers had been in a bad accident just outside the city, and I came along to see if you needed my help. It's just as well I did.

"Mr Hanley's injuries are only superficial, probably because he was sitting in the back seat. He could be discharged now but he won't leave till he knows that you're all right."

"Mr. Hanley?" Helena said vaguely, and a look of alarm came over Driffield's face.

"Don't tell me you've got amnesia?" he said. "Look, you've *got* to remember or I can't help you. Do you know your name?"

"Yes," she said after an agonized moment. "It's Helena Catesby. I work for Brian Hanley, and we came to Florence for the Design Fair." She recited the last words quickly, as though trying to get them out while she could still remember them.

Driffield's face relaxed slightly. "That's a relief. Now, I hope you can answer my next question. Where is your driver's license?"

"My what?"

"You were driving that car when it crashed," he said impatiently. "The police are going to want to see your license. I took the liberty of going through your bag but it isn't there. Where is it?"

"It's in England," she said faintly. "I didn't think I'd need it."

"Then why on earth did you drive?" Driffield demanded. "What were you thinking of?"

"I don't know," she said, bewildered. "I can't remember anything about the last part of the evening. I don't even remember getting into the car. I can't believe I did it."

"There's no doubt about it. You were behind the wheel when the accident occurred. The truck driver saw you there when he got out of the cab, and the police found you still sitting there. Now you say you weren't carrying a license.

"I'm afraid you may be in serious trouble, Mrs. Catesby. You were driving that car in what seems to have been a reckless fashion. In the truck driver's statement he said that you'd swerved wildly across the road into his path. If he hadn't managed to pull aside the accident would have been a great deal worse, and you all might have been killed.

"As it is, the girl who was in the car with you is on the critical list and I'm afraid her chances aren't good. She's also an Italian, which makes it a great deal worse for you. The Italians don't like foreigners coming into their country without proper documents and injuring their people." Driffield's manner had become perceptibly less friendly since finding out she wasn't carrying a license.

"Girl?" said Helena, confused. "What girl?"

"Mrs. Catesby," he said emphatically, "you'd been to a party, hadn't you?"

"Yes, that's right, I remember now. We met the girl at the party—"

"How much did you have to drink while you were there?" demanded Driffield.

"Not much. I don't remember exactly, but I never drink much."

She thought she heard him mutter, "That's what they all say," but she couldn't be sure. Her head was aching worse than ever and she closed her eyes.

"That is enough," came the nun's firm voice. "You will please leave now, *signore*. My patient must have some sleep before she has to talk to the police."

The voices grew fainter as the two moved toward the door, but in the stillness of the room Helena could clearly hear the nun say, "The consulate will help her, surely?" and Driffield's exasperated voice replying, "Naturally. We'll get her the very best lawyer in Florence. Brian Hanley is a British member of Parliament, and the last thing we want is any scandal attached to him. But you know as well as I do, Sister, that it's jail for what she's done. And if Lucilla Dorani dies it'll be a very long jail sentence; it could be up to ten years. It's going to take more than the efforts of the British consulate to prevent that. More like a miracle."

Helena heard the words but they didn't alarm her, because they didn't register as referring to herself. All sounds and impressions came from a distance, and at the door to her mind they fell back, defeated by the clamor that was already inside.

Brian was there in her head, a great laughing giant of a man, attractive in a blunt-featured way. Some Nordic ancestor had bequeathed him his blond, wavy hair and periwinkle-blue eyes that made him look younger than his forty-three years, and his charm still held a touch of the boyish. Helena had seen his charming side most often, because for the two years she had worked for him he'd been cheerfully trying to seduce her. When that failed, he'd hinted about marriage, and it was tacitly understood between them that soon the matter would be settled.

Helena was attracted by his easy good nature, although she knew it hid a touch of steel that surfaced now and then. With the aid of that steel he'd taken the nearly bankrupt leather-goods business his father had left him, shaken it by the scruff of its neck and transformed it into a prosperous, expanding concern. Then, bored by his success, he had looked around for new worlds to conquer.

For several years he'd been an active member of the local council, something that was always useful to a businessman. When the constituency's sitting M.P. decided to retire because of ill health, Brian charmed the party into choosing him as its candidate for the coming by-election. That had been a year ago, and for the past twelve months Brian Hanley, M.P., had divided his time between London and his constituency, which luckily wasn't too far away.

During the end of the long summer recess he'd said to Helena, "Let's take a trip to Florence. There's a Design Fair there in ten days, and as my designer you ought to go with me."

At first she'd refused, for she had her own reasons for wishing to avoid Florence. But when she reminded Brian what they were he had said impatiently, "Good grief, that was all over years ago, wasn't it? Don't be tiresome, darling. Florence is a major center for design and leather. You're not going to be much use as my designer if you refuse to go where the action is."

She had delayed giving him a final answer, hoping he would drop the idea. When he hadn't, she'd given in. After all, it *had* been ten years ago.

"But you don't need to go, surely?" she'd said. "Shouldn't you stay here, nursing the constituency?"

"The by-election was a year ago. What do I want to nurse the constituency for now? It's about time it was weaned, anyway. You can't expect me to pass up the chance of a trip alone with you, can you? Tax deductible as well."

He'd laughed and thrown his arm around her in the warmhearted way she found so endearing, and the matter had been settled with her doing what Brian wanted.

She wasn't in love with him, but she'd almost decided that when he finally asked her to marry him she would say yes. An engagement in her teens had ended in misery. In her twenties, three years of marriage to Gary Catesby had culminated in an acrimonious divorce. It all had left her wary of giving her heart. Next time round she'd be content with a marriage of common sense, and common sense dictated that she marry Brian, who was good-natured and would be an excellent father when their children came along. Theirs would never be a meeting of true minds, but he would make no demands on that secret inner part of herself that was still so rawly sensitive.

She'd accompanied him to Florence and, after the first pang at being back in the beautiful city that had once been the place of her dreams, had found that she was more at ease than she'd expected. She was so far removed now from the bright-faced, eager-eyed girl of seventeen who'd come here to study art; so much had happened since. The young, ecstatic ghost of herself that she'd dreaded seeing so much made only a brief appearance, and disappeared at her command.

There was another ghost, more accusing, less easily banished, but eventually even he was blotted out by the rush of events during those three days. Helena found the Design Fair genuinely fascinating and became so absorbed that Brian commented grumpily that he'd expected her to have *some* time for him. The car he'd rented in hopes of long sight-seeing drives to lonely places stood idly in the hotel parking lot.

But on the last evening he'd been able to drive it for a trip into the Tuscan hills, where a party was being held at the home of a fancy-goods manufacturer they'd met at the fair. Helena hadn't wanted to go. She was tired out and had been looking forward to a quiet dinner with Brian followed by an early night, alone. But Brian had sensed lucrative business and insisted that the two of them attend the party.

At this point her memory was thrown into utter confusion. Pictures and sounds came and went, eluding her frantic efforts to hold on to them. She was tired—there was a glass in her hand—Brian was saying, "Come on, darling, enjoy yourself." There was a girl—Lucilla, was that her name? She'd had a willful, petulant face.

How had the party ended? Why had she been driving the car? Desperately she tried to pierce the thick fog that surrounded the end of the evening. She *must* remember! That man had said a jail sentence, but it couldn't be true. Surely she hadn't done anything wrong! But her memory remained frighteningly silent, and refused to acquit her.

By turning her head she could just see the edge of her handbag protruding from the shelf of the bedside cabinet. She managed to raise herself on one elbow and stretch toward it. Her body ached with every movement, but she could tell now that nothing was broken. At last she grasped the bag and drew it toward her. She had a vague, illogical feeling that if she could see what she looked like she'd know how bad everything was.

As soon as she'd extracted the mirror and peered into it she knew that by this yardstick she was in a very bad way. Her face was bleached so white that it seemed to merge with the bandage around her head. The scratches and bruises stood out starkly against that unnatural pallor, and her eyes were sunk in shadow.

It was a face that normally looked younger than its twenty-seven years: The bloom of health could make the fair skin glow with warmth and the thick, red-gold hair shine wherever the light touched its waves. But now what she could see of her hair was lank and lifeless, and her eyes were dull as they stared back at her. They were deep brown, startlingly dark against her fair coloring, and they usually made heads turn, though she wasn't a beauty. Her fine-drawn features were good, but the dominant effect of her face was of a lively, sparkling intelligence. Only those intense, lustrous eyes sometimes gave her the illusion of beauty. But the illusion had gone now.

She put the mirror away and fell back. At last she slid into an unquiet sleep in which she never stopped being conscious of the pain in her head. Once she groaned and was aware of the sound being smothered by lips lightly brushing hers. When she opened her eyes Brian was sitting beside her. He looked pale and there was a large bruise on one side of his head, but he had plainly sustained no major injury.

"Brian," she said eagerly, "thank God you're all right!"

"Poor little girl," he said in a kindly voice that comforted her, "you've been through the wars, haven't you? That was a pretty nasty bash you got on your head."

"What about the other girl, the one who was in the car with us?"

"Lucilla Dorani. I'm afraid she's in pretty bad condition. She's still unconscious, but don't give up hope. She'll pull through. They're very tough in this part of the world."

The glib categorizing grated on her, but she feared to question him further about Lucilla. She was alive. That was the main thing.

"Brian, just how much trouble am I in?" she asked, a bit nervously. "Mr Driffield said something about jail. It can't be true, can it?"

A shadow crossed his face. "The courts are much tougher on drunken driving here than in England, Helena. If you're convicted it's a mandatory sentence of four years."

"What?" she cried frantically. "But Brian, it isn't true. I wasn't drunk, you know I wasn't. I hardly ever drink anything—"

"Hush." He took hold of her and forced her gently back onto the bed. "Please, sweetie, don't get excited. You'll hurt yourself. I don't know exactly what you had to drink, but it was more than usual. You said you were worn out and wanted something to perk you up, but you didn't seem to eat much. Alcohol's deadly on an empty stomach, especially if you're tired. Oh, God—" he ran a hand distractedly through his hair "—I feel so much to blame for making you go to that damn party. You warned me that you were exhausted. If it hadn't been for that you'd never have drunk so much."

"So much?" she echoed in horror. "Just how much did I have?"

"I told you, I don't know exactly. We weren't together all the time, but whenever I saw you, you seemed to have a different glass in your hand, so I guess you were mixing them."

"But how did I end up driving the car?" she said, wondering how much worse this could get.

He gave her a distracted look. "Don't you remember any details?"

"Nothing after about halfway through the evening. I don't recall how we left the villa or anything. Please, Brian, tell me the worst."

"I'd taken my jacket off. When I collected it at the end of the evening the car keys weren't in my pocket. You'd taken them. I thought it was a joke at first, but you were determined to drive. I tried to talk you out of it but you got into the driver's seat and wouldn't budge. I had to give in.

"I wasn't too worried at that point. Apart from insisting on driving, you seemed all right. But when you started off I knew you were worse than you seemed. You were swerving all over the place. I tried to make you stop and let me take over but you wouldn't listen. I couldn't insist because I was in the back seat.

Lucilla had got in front before I could stop her. If I'd been beside you I might have risked grabbing the wheel. As it was, I didn't dare."

"Why was Lucilla in the car with us?"

"The boyfriend who'd taken her to the party had simply dumped her and gone off with another girl. She was frantic to get home on time because her family didn't know where she was. She's very young, and she kept on and on about what would happen to her if someone called Guido found out. I suppose he must be her brother or something. From the way she talked he sounded a real domestic tyrant, so I took pity on her and said we'd give her a lift. I wish to God I hadn't now. When that truck appeared I think you got confused. We'd have been all right if you'd kept going straight, but you were still swerving about and you went right into his path."

"Yes, I remember that in a vague way," she said with an effort. "Everything else is a blank, but I can recall that last split second. The wheel seemed to come alive and I just couldn't control it. I know I never meant to turn into the truck's path."

"You must have been trying to turn away and got confused," he said sympathetically. "Foreign cars and foreign roads can be a nightmare. It wasn't your fault, darling."

"But it *was*," she said frantically. "I shouldn't have been driving. If that girl dies...Brian, how bad is she?"

He took a ragged breath. "The collision was on her side of the car," he said. "She was hit worse than either of us."

Helena stared at him in horror, longing for some sign of hope to cling to. But Brian's haggard eyes told her the worst, and she covered her face with her hands.

The door opened and the nun came quickly into the room. "You must go, *signore*," she said. "The police wish to speak with Signora Catesby and it is better if they do not find you here."

"I'm not going," said Brian firmly. "Helena needs me—"

"*Signore*, please, you can do her no good by remaining here. Also they will be angry that I let you in first," the nun pleaded. "I should not have done that."

Brian grimaced. "I hate leaving you," he said to Helena.

She squeezed his hand, feeling stronger for his loyalty. She was closer to loving him at that moment than she had ever been.

"You must go," she said urgently. "You can come back afterward."

He kissed her and departed. The policeman entered a few moments later. Helena had had time to compose herself and stave off some of the apprehension that was gradually taking possession of her. Things were no longer happening at a distance. Everything was here and now. She was in desperate trouble, facing a prison sentence, and she couldn't even remember what she'd done.

Sergeant Callini looked like a fundamentally kind man, but his face was set in stern lines. He apologized for troubling Helena while she was feeling badly, but he had to hear what she had to say as soon as possible. She told her story as far as she could, but when she came to the last part of the evening and heard herself repeating "I don't know—I can't remember—" again and again, her nervousness began to rise.

The sergeant heard her denials impassively and noted them all down. Once he looked up from his notebook and stared at her hard, and Helena had a weird sensation that someone had thrown a spotlight on her. In its light she could see herself as she must seem to this man, a careless drunk who had risked other people's lives, and now was hiding behind a lapse of memory. But all he said was, "It's not uncommon, after an incident of this nature, for the few hours immediately beforehand to be blotted out. Gradually the memory returns. For your sake, *signora*, I hope it happens quickly. You may remember something that will improve your position.

"I must tell you that at the moment your position is very serious. On your own admission you were driving while not in possession of a license. Your reckless driving caused an accident, and there is evidence to suggest that you were not sober. Lucilla Dorani's condition is critical. If she dies, then to a charge of drunken and careless driving will be added one of manslaughter."

Helena stared at him wild-eyed, unable to speak. This was a nightmare and at any moment she would wake up. But the silence stretched on and on, and she did not wake.

"I won't attempt to have you removed from this hospital until the doctors say that it is safe to do so," the policeman went on. "But you must realize that from this moment you are under arrest on a charge of drunken driving. Other charges may be added later. When you are improved you will go to the Women's House Of Detention to await a formal hearing."

She caught her breath. "But—isn't there any bail?" she stammered.

"In this country the accused can sometimes be given 'provisional liberty,'" said the Sergeant. "But it depends on the circumstances. Where evidence is lacking, perhaps—but there is a great deal of evidence against you, I'm afraid. Also, you might try to leave the country, so the court would ask for a guarantor, some respected Florentine citizen, who would be responsible for you." His face softened slightly. "Do you know anyone in Florence who might be prepared to help you?"

Her mind flew to the one person in Florence that she knew, a man who hated her and would rejoice over her present agony. If Valerio Lucci had planned his revenge he could not have chosen better than this.

"No," she said bleakly, "I have no friends in Florence."

When the sergeant had gone Helena lay staring at the ceiling, trying to fight down the tide of panic that threatened to engulf her. She longed for Brian's comforting presence. She hadn't realized before how strong and loyal he could be in a crisis, but now she knew he was the one person she had to cling to in a terrifying world. If she could just see him again, hear his affectionate voice and feel the reassurance of his kiss, she knew she could cope. Her heart leaped with relief as the nun returned.

"Sister," she said eagerly, "I must see Mr. Hanley again. Please, will you find him for me?"

But the sister shook her head regretfully. "It is not possible," she said. "I am under orders not to let him return."

"But you let him come in before," Helena pleaded.

"But then you weren't under arrest. Now that you've been arrested, you are officially in police custody, although you will remain here. Please, *signora*, try to understand. Mr. Hanley can't visit you any more than he could if you were in a cell."

The word *cell* brought the dreadful reality of her position home to Helena like the last nail being hammered into a coffin. The arrest had turned the little hospital ward into a jail, and she was as much a prisoner as if there were bars on the window.

"Do you mean," she asked, in a voice that was barely steady, "that I'm allowed no visitors at all?"

"Oh, no—" the sister's face brightened with relief at being able to offer a small crumb of comfort "—you may see Mr. Driffield from the consulate, and also your lawyer. You may be sure they will do their best for you. Mr. Driffield promised that you would have the best lawyer in Florence."

"Will you promise to let me know if Lucilla Dorani—that is…"

"I'll tell you if there is any change in her condition," said the sister sympathetically. She looked up as a man in a white coat appeared in the doorway. He nodded to them both and stepped up to the bed.

"I am Dr. Polione," he said. "I'm glad to see that you have recovered consciousness, *signora*."

The doctor remained with Helena for several minutes. He seemed satisfied with her condition, assured her that her amnesia for the few hours before the accident would probably be temporary and declared that she would be up and about in a few days. Helena could take no comfort from this cheerful report, as it meant only that the day when she would be taken to jail was closer.

As soon as the door had closed behind the two of them Helena began to shake. There was nothing to save her from the horror that was taking control of her mind. She knew now that she wasn't going to wake from the nightmare. She must live it through till the end, and the end might mean a death on her conscience and years in a foreign prison.

She tried to force herself to remain calm. She'd always been proud of her strength and decisiveness, but never before had she felt so desolate and lonely—or so thoroughly frightened. She pressed her hands over her face, and turned her head so that she could burrow into the pillow. Now nothing could silence the dry, ugly sobs that convulsed her, and she gave way to them.

When she had cried herself out she lay quietly, exhausted and drained of everything but despair. She had only one hope left— the unknown lawyer who would soon be coming to see her. And that was really no hope at all, for what could even the best lawyer do in the face of the damning facts? Yet despite this reasoning her mind seized on the thought of the lawyer. He was her last chance—a slim one perhaps, but the only one she had.

A faint noise made her realize that she was no longer alone. She drew her hands away from her face and saw a man standing just inside the door. He was in his midthirties, with pale, lean features and a firm mouth. His dark, classically tailored suit proclaimed him a professional man, and his leather briefcase, clasped in long, tense fingers, confirmed that impression.

But Helena saw only his face. It was a face she knew. But the dark eyes that had once shone with adoration for her now held a stern, set expression that made her quail.

"Valerio," she whispered, "what are you doing here?"

"I'm here at the request of the British consulate, *signora*. I was informed that two Britishers had been involved in a car accident, and that my services as a lawyer were required because one of them was facing serious charges."

"Oh, yes, you're a lawyer—I'd forgotten..." she murmured, trying frantically to get her bearings.

Valerio Lucci came into the room and drew up a chair beside the bed. There was a wintry smile on his face, but he didn't look directly at her as he seated himself and said, "There is, of course, no reason why you should have remembered anything about me. Trivial matters don't remain long in the mind. May we get down to business at once? It is essential that I know all you can remember."

"Valerio, wait—please. I must get this clear. How can you possibly want to help me? Or have *you* forgotten?"

Now Valerio Lucci raised his head and looked straight at her, his eyes hard and remote as stones. "I can assure you, *signora*, that I recall all the essential details of our previous acquaintance. We met ten years ago, in this city. We fell in love—at any rate, that's what I believed had happened. You promised to marry me. On our wedding day I went to the church and waited more than an hour before facing the fact that you had no intention of arriving.

"Now, if you are feeling strong enough, I should like to go over the details of your case."

Two

Some love affairs begin with moonlight and music. Theirs had begun with an execution.

Helena James had been seventeen when she came to Florence to study art. She'd known beyond any shadow of doubt that her fingers had the true gift of creation, if only she could learn how to focus it. Whether to be a painter or a sculptor had been the burning question in her life in those days. Perhaps she would be both.

"After all," she'd said with the blazing confidence of extreme youth, "Michelangelo did both."

At the Florence academy she would develop her talents in both directions. After that it was only a matter of time before she became world-famous. At seventeen this logical progression had simply seemed inevitable.

There'd been no opposition from home when she proposed leaving England to study in a foreign country. Helena's mother was dead and her father, though fond of his daughter in the abstract, was always slightly nonplussed by her in the flesh.

He'd recently remarried, and the hostility between Helena and his new wife had helped to make the trip to Florence seem like an excellent idea. He'd supervised his daughter's arrangements with great efficiency, for his touch was as sure when dealing with practical matters as it was unsure when dealing with people, but when he had satisfied himself that she was staying at a respectable hostel and knew the telephone number of the British consulate, he'd let her go with barely disguised relief. Her stepmother had been frankly glad to be rid of her.

From the first moment she was totally happy at the academy. She was where she'd dreamed of being since she'd been given her first box of crayons as a four-year-old and known that this was what she had been made for. She'd bent all her energies toward this ambition, studying subjects that would be of the greatest use to her. These had included languages, and she arrived in Italy speaking excellent Italian.

She soon found that this wasn't enough. To live in Florence she also needed to understand the robust Tuscan dialect, and she set to work to master this too, aided by a naturally good ear. She was never short of willing teachers, for her eager vivacity and merry eyes were like magnets to the men around her.

One of the men who never joined her crowd was Valerio Lucci. She first noticed him because he was older than the other students. Her guess was that he must be thirty. Later she discovered that he was only twenty-five. He seemed older because of his air of settled gravity and the extreme reserve of his manner.

He wasn't there during her first term, but when she returned after the Christmas holiday she found that he'd joined the twice-weekly class on the history of art. These were the only times she ever saw him; he was evidently not a full-time student. But at the Wednesday and Friday history class he was almost always there, sitting a little apart from the other students, occasionally asking a question in a quiet voice.

Sometimes Helena had caught his eyes on her, dark, intense and serious. They were beautiful eyes, she'd realized, and they made her wonder how he'd look if he smiled. She began to study his face, watching for a smile. But she watched in vain, and one day he looked up too quickly for her to glance away. She turned her head, embarrassed to have been caught staring, and furiously aware that she was blushing like a schoolgirl. But that evening, when she and a crowd of friends had repaired to the local coffee and wine bar, Valerio joined them for the first time.

Even then he didn't sit at the same table, but at the next one, where he could watch and listen while still remaining apart. She'd been practicing her Tuscan, floundering over a new word, unsure of its meaning but confused by three different translations she'd been offered. At last Valerio had leaned across and said, "The word means none of these things. They are making fun of you, *signorina*."

Gravely he had explained the word's true meaning. It was slightly indecent, and she realized the extent of the joke that the others had been enjoying at her expense. But she managed to laugh and say, "I'll get my own back some time."

She wanted to thank Valerio but he'd already turned back to his book, ignoring the cries of "spoilsport" from the other men, as though they were flies beneath his notice. When the rest of the crowd rose to go Valerio never moved, but Helena's sharp eyes noticed something in the tense set of his shoulder muscles, and she had a sudden conviction that he was waiting to see if she left with the others. She had half risen, but impulsively she sat down again. Only when they were alone did Valerio look up. "You will permit me to buy you a coffee, *signorina*?" he said formally.

"Thank you. I'd love one." She waited while he gave the order to a waiter, then said, "I'm glad you stepped in when you did. I don't mind being teased, but—"

"But that joke was going a little far," he agreed. "They're a good crowd, but they tend to get rowdy if they think they can get away with it. They find it entertaining to embarrass a young girl."

"Well, they're harmless," she said with a shrug. "And as I said, I'll have the laugh on them yet."

"I've no doubt that you will. You're always laughing. I have observed you. You're to be envied; to be light of heart is a great gift."

"I thought you disapproved. I've seen you frowning at me."

"No, I don't disapprove. I don't have the gift of lightheartedness myself, but I like to see it in others—especially in you. You are enchanting when you laugh."

He said these words with no departure from his quiet manner, and it was a moment before Helena realized that he'd paid her a compliment. She didn't know what to say, and was glad when he went on talking.

"You're very young to be living alone in a foreign city. I've heard that you have no friends or family here."

A more experienced woman would have picked up the hint that he had been asking people about her, but she merely answered innocently, "I live in a hostel, but I'm not alone. It's a terribly respectable place. My father made sure of that. And it's run by a fearsomely strict woman. We call her 'the dragon.'"

He encouraged her to talk and before long she'd poured out her whole life story. He was easy to talk to because he seemed to be fascinated by every word she said. And all the time he kept his eyes fixed earnestly on her face, with an expression in them that she had never seen in any man's eyes before. She didn't know whether she liked it or not.

He took her to dinner, and she went on talking to him. As the evening wore on she grew more aware of the unfathomable look in his eyes. She felt shivers go up her spine, which resembled the ones she'd felt in awkward, experimental kisses with boyfriends, except that these were much more intense. Yet Valerio Lucci wasn't kissing her. He wasn't even touching her. Through the evening his fingers only brushed her once, when he handed her formally to her chair, and then he showed no inclination to let them linger—as she wished he would.

The last thought was formed before she could catch it back, and left her amazed at herself. She began to anticipate the end of the evening, when surely Valerio would kiss her good-night. But he only showed her to the door of the hostel, bade her farewell and departed. She was left with a feeling of letdown. But then she reminded herself that he couldn't possibly have kissed her there where there was danger of the dragon seeing them, and that made her feel better.

She wondered how he would behave toward her when he arrived for the Friday afternoon lecture. But when the time came there was no sign of him. She shrugged the matter off, though inwardly dismayed and surprised at the depths of her own disappointment. She began counting the days before he might appear again, then stopped herself firmly.

He was back the following week, and again he asked her to dinner. She accepted, promising herself that she wouldn't mention his disappearance, but as soon as they were seated she found herself asking, "What happened to you last week? You missed your lecture."

"I'm unable to attend as often as I should like. I am a lawyer, and last Friday my presence was required in court. It is unfortunate, but it cannot be helped. Luckily the principal of the academy is an old friend of my father, and he is understanding about my situation."

"But you're never going to get anywhere if you miss half the lectures. If you want to take art seriously why don't you just give up being a lawyer? Or perhaps—" she scowled at him as a suspicion crossed her mind "—perhaps you're not taking it seriously."

Not to take art seriously was the worst crime in the world, and some of her hostility showed in her voice. He gave a very faint smile and hastened to reassure her.

"Nothing would please me more than to be able to spend all my time at the academy, as you do. But it isn't possible. I have to stay a lawyer."

"Why?" A dreadful possibility occurred to her. "You're not—I mean, you don't have a—a family to support?"

He came to her rescue. "No, I'm not married," he assured her. "If I had a wife, you and I wouldn't be spending this evening together. But I promised my father that I would enter the family law firm, and I can't go back on my word.

"I'm his only surviving son. My older brother, Oliviero, was going to join my father in the firm, which would have left me free to follow my own wishes and become an art dealer. But Oliviero died in the terrible floods of 1966, and my father made me promise that I would take his place."

"But that's antiquated," she'd protested. "You're entitled to live your own life your own way."

"Ah, yes," he said in his soft voice, "I know that theory. We all do what we want and never mind the feelings of anybody else. But I cannot live that way. It's not the way I was raised. My family have been lawyers for three hundred years, and for most of that time we have occupied the same offices.

"I'm an Italian, Helena. With us the family is all-important. It meant the world to my father that he had a son to follow him in our firm. When he asked me to give up my own wishes for the sake of the family I had no choice but to agree.

"Besides, I haven't lost everything. I can still study art and collect it in my spare time. In a limited way I may even do some dealing. I can combine that with the law."

She'd shaken her head at that. She was young, and passionate about everything. In her black-and-white view it just wasn't possible for a man to give up something he truly cared about for an abstract concept like duty. Valerio, she decided, was deficient in true feeling, otherwise he would have followed his heart.

She realized that he was watching her with a gleam of amusement in his eyes, and she had an uncomfortable feeling that he'd guessed her thoughts.

"It must be a dreadful life, always having to do your duty and never think of yourself," she said.

"On the contrary. It saves a great deal of inconvenience and having a guilty conscience," he asserted, still with that hint of amusement that disconcerted her.

"Well, I couldn't do it. Not over big things. I should simply live my life the way *I* wanted, and never mind what anyone else thought."

"I don't think you are as selfish as you would like me to believe. At seventeen one likes to pretend to have all the vices, only to discover later that one has some quite unexpected virtues after all. It is very disappointing."

She had to laugh at the droll tone of his voice. It was a revelation to her that his gravity could be shot through with this quiet humor. At the same time it annoyed her that he spoke as though he came from an older generation. She knew by now that he was only eight years her senior. But Valerio was old for his age. Probably, she thought in a mischievous moment, his mind had been ten years old on the day he was born. At any rate, his seriousness seemed to be an intrinsic part of him. She, on the other hand, was beginning to have a depressing suspicion that she was young for her age.

The sweetness of their friendship made her life in Florence perfect. She told herself that she regarded him as a kind of uncle. No other attitude was possible with a man who maintained such a strict distance between them. For even after that first night, when other opportunities had presented themselves, he had made no move to kiss her. By now Helena was beginning to fear that he didn't intend to. She enjoyed their twice-weekly dinners and the long talks in which he encouraged her to open her mind. At those times she discovered in herself a fluency and a profundity of thought that she had never suspected she possessed.

At the lectures they both attended he didn't make her conspicuous by always sitting beside her. Often they would be on opposite sides of the room, and she liked this because it gave her the chance to study him. She enjoyed watching his lean, handsome features and the dark eyes that sometimes seemed alive with an inner light.

He was a tall man, and his slender build made him seem even more so. Helena would find her eyes wandering uncontrollably over him, noticing the sudden strain of the thin material of his shirt against the firm flesh beneath, the grace of his movements, particularly the gestures of his long, nervous hands.

She was too inexperienced for her senses to have been roused. She had never desired a man before, and didn't recognize her desire for what it was. She longed to kiss the firm, beautifully shaped lips and feel his strong hands holding her. Beyond that she knew only a vague unsatisfied yearning.

Valerio haunted her thoughts when she went home to England for the Easter break. She was consumed with curiosity about him and longed to penetrate the guard of quiet courtesy that he kept constantly in place. When she returned to Florence to begin her third term her eyes immediately sought him out.

She spent her weekends wandering the city's many art galleries. Her favorite was the Palazzo Vecchio, which was the oldest palace in Florence, and once its seat of government. Now it housed many of Italy's greatest pictures and statues. One Saturday afternoon she encountered Valerio, and she let him guide her to his favorite pictures, for he was an excellent teacher and she enjoyed listening to him.

Then they went out and sat at a table in one of the open-air cafés of the Piazza della Signoria. It was May. Summer's heat had already begun and they were both in light clothing. The sleeves of Valerio's white shirt were pushed back to the elbows, showing smooth brown skin. Even casually dressed he contrived to look elegant. Watching his gestures, and the turn of his black head as he talked to the waiter, Helena realized that he never made a move that wasn't graceful. In her own jeans and old shirt she felt like a ragamuffin beside him.

Over coffee they continued their lively discussion about the pictures they'd just seen. Gradually the conversation left artists of the past and came round to artists of the present, and at last he asked her what she intended to do when she'd finished her two years at the academy.

"I'm not too sure," she said. "I can't go back to my father's home. It just wouldn't work out. I have a few thousand pounds my mother left me. I'd thought of trying to live on that till I got a start, but I don't know how long it would last."

"But what do you hope to do in the end?" he persisted, frowning.

"Be a very great artist, that's all. I've quite made up my mind I'm not going to get sidetracked into an auction house or designing patterns for china or—or illustrating books. I'm going to paint great pictures."

But he shook his head and said firmly, "No, you must put that thought out of your head. You'll never be great in the sense that you mean."

She stared at him dumbfounded, for despite the austerity of his nature she knew that he wasn't an unkind man.

"You've only seen a very little of my work, just a few sketches," she said at last. "Surely that's a rather premature judgment?"

"I'm not judging by your work, but by yourself," he replied. "Your drawing is excellent. You have a real gift for conveying movement, and you can capture a likeness. You might be a successful portrait painter, but you'll never reach the heights you dream of because you lack one essential quality. And that is detachment."

She was too surprised to say anything, but could only sit gazing at him, waiting for him to continue. After a moment, he did. "Have you ever wondered why the giants of painting are men?" he said. "There is a reason, and it isn't just a chauvinistic one. The fact is that an artist can only portray the world if he has the detachment to stand back from it."

"But surely he ought to care—" she began to argue with him.

"To care, yes, but not to become too deeply involved. It's like a monk who must love all his fellow creatures, but in a such a general way that no individual among them feels his love as a personal thing. The artist must care about the world before he can show it to itself. But if he cares too much about any one part of it he will lose his sense of perspective, and his mirror will become distorted. Then his greatness is at an end."

"But there have been great women painters," she insisted. "What about Gwen John? Or are you going to claim that she wasn't so good?"

He smiled faintly at her fierce tone. "No, I would place her among the best, infinitely better than her brother Augustus. But she only proves my point. She had detachment. She ended her life as a hermit in a remote village in France. Eminent men came to visit her, and she refused to open her door to them. Her inner vision absorbed her to the point that though she lived *in* the world she was not *of* the world.

"But Gwen John was unique. This kind of detachment happens mostly among men. In women it is almost unknown. You, my Helena, with your warm, overflowing heart, would have opened the door and invited everyone in for a party."

"But you're quibbling about details," she said, trying not to show the little stab of pleasure she'd felt at his casually possessive "my Helena." "She was just being unsociable."

"Very well, I will give you an example of real detachment. Next time we come to the Palazzo Vecchio I will point out to you the window where they executed Bernardo Baroncelli in 1478. He had conspired against the Medici and they hanged him from a window of the palace. As his body swung to and fro a young artist called Leonardo da Vinci stood below, making a detailed sketch of it."

"Ugh!"

"I entirely agree. But that is detachment."

"I don't believe it. It's just one of those stories—"

"No, truly. The sketch still exists. The original is in France, but I have a reproduction in my own home, if you would care to see it."

She accepted at once. She was curious to see the home of this man who fascinated and intrigued her. Perhaps within his own four walls she could learn something about him.

They drove down toward the river Arno, to that section of the city where lawyers' offices have clustered together for hundreds of years in the shadow of the city prison. The Bargello is a prison no more, but the lawyers remain. Valerio briefly pointed out the door that led to his own office. It was narrow and discreetly shabby, and normally Helena would never have noticed it.

Then he had swung the car into one of the little winding side streets and stopped. He took her hand to guide her up the little dark staircase to his apartment on the second floor. When his front door had closed behind them he stood without moving, looking at her, his eyes dark and troubled. She met his gaze, feeling something pounding in her throat. The sensation seemed to spread over her whole body, and she could no longer breath properly. Then suddenly he took a step toward her, and in another moment they were in each other's arms.

She clung to him, eagerly raising her face for his kiss. It was long and deep, and exceeded her wildest imaginings. Nothing that had ever happened before in her short life had prepared her for the shattering effect of his lips on hers. She wanted to kiss him forever, and sighed with disappointment when he drew away.

"I've wanted to kiss you from the very first day," he said in a brooding voice, still holding her. "Since then, I don't think there has been an hour, or a moment when I have not tried to imagine what it would feel like to have you in my arms."

"I'm so glad," she said happily. "I thought I was the only one who felt like that."

He smiled at the passionate eagerness in her voice, but she didn't see it. She was still in his arms, her head on his shoulder, listening to the swift beat of his heart.

"But now," he continued, his voice hoarse, "I think you must go away."

"*No!*" Her cry of wild protest startled him and he drew back to look into her face.

"Helena, listen to me, please. I had no right to bring you here. It was wrong of me. You're a child, you know nothing—"

"I know that I want you!"

Even then it was the voice of a child that spoke, a child determined to have what she'd set her heart on. Somewhere deep within himself he knew this, but his blood was pounding at the nearness of her, blotting out rational thought. He made one last attempt. "Darling," he said in a desperate voice, "let me send you away while there's still time...."

But even as he said it he knew there was no time. The fresh, sweet smell of her was in his nostrils, turning his limbs to water. When her slim arms, strong with the strength of youth and passion, slid around his neck, he knew he was lost.

Helena was aware only of the blissful sense of doing something that was utterly right and perfect. She was full of joy in his arms, every inch of her burning with the desire for his touch. She cut off his tortured words by pulling his head down to hers and seeking his mouth with her own, knowing instinctively that he no longer had the strength or the will to resist her.

It began as her kiss, but gradually she felt him move to take command, turning her gently against him so that he could cradle her head against his shoulder and hold her in a crushing embrace. She was content to follow his lead, letting her lips fall softly apart at the urgent pressure of his tongue. She felt dizzy at the sensation as he invaded her, teasing the inside of her mouth with flickering movements.

She felt his fingers fumbling with the pins in her hair. Then it was loose, cascading about her shoulders. He tore his mouth from hers and began raining kisses over her face and neck, his hands caressing the mass of red-gold waves.

He began to open the buttons of her shirt, one by one. She was embarrassed suddenly for her shabby old clothes, but the feeling was swept away in the waves of physical excitement that were surging over her. And she was joyfully aware that when her clothes had been thrown aside there was nothing shabby about the gift she would give him. Her body was young and beautiful and perfect for his loving.

Her heartbeat quickened as he pulled open the last button and tossed her shirt aside. He removed her tiny bra in a moment, revealing small, uptilted breasts that he touched reverently. She blushed, for no man had seen her naked before, and she was embarrassed at the way her excitement plainly showed in the taut, rosy nipples.

Valerio seemed to understand because he said softly, "Come," and took her hand to lead her into the bedroom. To her great relief he pulled the shutters almost closed, so that only a little light crept into the room. She turned her back on him to remove the rest of her clothes, and when she looked toward him again he was already under the covers. He pushed them back and held out his arms to her.

As soon as she was in the bed he pulled her close to him, and she realized that he was as naked as herself. She could see nothing, but she could feel the length of him against her, his firm, lean flesh pressed against her soft body, and involuntarily she shivered at the unaccustomed sensation.

But his hands touched her in leisurely fashion, giving her the time she needed to relax and abandon herself to the delicious warmth that was beginning to suffuse her. He made no demands, but lured her on with gentle caresses of his long, nervous fingers. She scarcely realized that the caresses were growing more intimate as he lovingly beguiled her to passion. She only knew that all her sensations had become mysteriously heightened, and concentrated in him.

She gave a sigh of blissful acceptance, rejoicing in each new sensation, savoring everything that was happening to her. He heard the sigh and smiled at her. It was unlike any smile she had seen from him before. It was warm and brilliant with happiness, as though it sprang from a light that glowed in his heart. It was the smile she had always longed to see on his face, but she hadn't known it until now.

"I have dreamed of you," he whispered, "but you are even more beautiful."

His hand was softly fondling one breast as he spoke, and she scarcely heard his words through the delight that flooded her. She moaned and writhed against him, and at once his head dropped and his lips seized the other nipple, teasing it tenderly, sending little electric shocks through her.

A slow throb was beginning to pervade her loins. Valerio had moved half across her, and she gasped as she became aware of his hard maleness, aroused and taut, urgently ready to claim her. The inside of her thighs ached to feel him there, to welcome him. But he made her wait while he teased her into a fury of anticipation with the exploration of his hands that caressed, enfolded, tantalized with devastating effect.

At last he slipped a knee between her legs and the weight of his body pressed down on hers. She looked up at his face hovering above hers, her eyes shining with a trust and eagerness that went to his heart. She felt the urgent, probing pressure as he sought her, found her, united himself with her. Waves of sweet shock went through her as he pierced the heart of her passion again and again. She moved in his rhythm, happy and confident in the arms of the man she loved. He made slow, deep thrusts inside her, and with each one she mounted higher in the crescendo of pleasure that was taking her toward the unknown pinnacle for which she yearned, yet which still eluded her.

"Slowly, my darling, give yourself time," the words were in her ear, full of fond indulgence for her eagerness. But there was no time. Life was short and there were so many things she wanted to do. So she hurried forward, reaching out young, anxious hands, lest the magic slip away before she had fully tasted it.

His movements became faster, more urgent. She responded avidly, conscious of blazing need exploding into fulfillment. Uncontrollable tremors convulsed her, draining her of strength, of will, of everything except passionate longing for this to go on for ever.

She became aware that the tumult in her blood was subsiding and she was lying in Valerio's arms, her nose buried against him, savoring the pleasant smell of sun and warmth that he carried with him. She had come down to earth again and found it an entirely different place.

He rose on one elbow and looked down at her. Gradually his face relaxed as he read the blissful message in hers, and he gave her the same happy smile as before. She took his face in her hands, lost in the wonder of him and of herself, and of what had happened between them. Over his shoulder she could see a gap in the shutters, and through it the branches of a tree that grew outside. They were laden with pink, luxurious blossoms, which seemed at this moment to be a part of her enveloping happiness. She had discovered love in the springtime of the year, in the springtime of her life, and found it to be perfect.

"To think you wanted to send me away," she said blissfully.

"It is what I should have done. But I've resisted you for so long, heart of my heart. I couldn't resist you any longer."

"Heart of my heart." She echoed the words in delight.

"It is what you are to me. Did you not know?"

"How could I? You were always so grave and stern."

"I cannot help it. It is my nature. But not with you. You know that now."

He said these words in his habitual serious manner, and once this would have fooled her. But she was beginning to know him. She had gained her first glimpse of the passionate depths of feeling that he kept concealed behind a reserved exterior. There was delight in the knowledge that for her he would lay aside the mask he wore for the rest of the world.

She pushed back the quilt and looked down at their naked limbs entwined, the roundness of her contours contrasting starkly with his firm, lean outline. Valerio's build was slight. Except for his height he was not a big man, but the arms around her had the sinewy strength of steel. She pressed her hands against his smooth chest, and at once he divined the game she was playing and tensed his muscles to hold her. Without moving he held her in an unbreakable grip. She could have fought him to the limit of her strength and he wouldn't even have noticed. After a few moments she gave up, laughing.

"That is nature's way," said Valerio with grave humor. "Woman is fickle, so man is made strong that he may keep her beside him."

"But I'm not fickle," she whispered, entranced. "I'll never leave you."

"Stay with me always, heart of my heart."

She repeated the words "heart of my heart" to herself while she dressed, lost in wonder and happiness. Valerio went into the kitchen to make some coffee and she had leisure to look around his apartment. It was a compact abode, dark with much wood panneling, and masculine looking. Some of the walls were covered with old, faded tapestries and on others hung pictures, the beginning of Valerio's collection.

The bed where they had lain was large and made of brass, with a patchwork counterpane flung over it. She straightened this, then let her eyes wander around the room. As she would have expected with Valerio, it was extremely neat and tidy. The one thing that surprised her slightly was the dressing table, which was covered with photographs in beautiful antique-silver frames. Valerio came in with the coffee while she was studying them.

"Those are my parents," he said, pointing to a middle-aged couple. "My father is dead now, but my mother is alive. This old couple here are my mother's parents, and these are my father's parents. Of these only my father's mother still lives." He indicated an old lady with a robust, cheerful face and a gleam in her eyes. "It's a joke in our family to say that my grandmother will live forever because St. Peter is too afraid of her to let her into heaven." He was smiling as he spoke, and his voice was vibrant with affection.

"Is she very fearsome?" said Helena, watching him.

"She is the kindest, warmest-hearted person in the world," he said emphatically, "but she is very decisive in everything she does, and that makes people nervous. In some ways you remind me of her."

"Don't tell me you're afraid of me." Helena chuckled.

"No, but then I'm one of the few people who doesn't fear my grandmother either—except when she's determined to do something for my own good. Then even I tend to flee for my life."

She laughed and pointed to another photograph, which showed a young man of barely twenty. "Who's that?"

"That was my brother Oliviero, of whom I told you. He died in the floods of sixty-six."

"Yes, I remember. And the little girl?"

"That is my sister Serena. She's just ten years old. You will meet her soon—" he caught Helena's eyes on him and colored "—that is, if you wish."

"Of course." There was nothing else to say, but she was startled. She knew that no Italian man would take a girl home to his family unless his intentions were deadly serious. At the same time she had a puzzled feeling that Valerio had said more than he had intended.

But one thing she understood very clearly. This was Valerio's world, containing just the few people that he loved and with whom he felt safe enough to reveal the warmer side of his personality, which he guarded so carefully behind a high, protective wall. For many weeks he had kept her just the other side of that wall, but today it had fallen, all in a moment. Suddenly she found herself confronting the real man, a man whose inner self was so vulnerable that it must be hidden behind defenses.

She saw that other self now as he turned to her and said abruptly, "Tell me that you are all right. Tell me that I haven't hurt or frightened you."

"How can you ask that?" she chided him. "You can see how happy I am."

But he wouldn't be put off. "Tell me," he insisted. "I must hear you say it."

"Valerio, you needn't worry about me," she said, half laughing, half dismayed. "I've never been happier in my life."

"I can't forget how trustingly you came to me, how brave and certain you were."

"I knew what I was doing."

He smiled and stroked her face. "You are never so young as when you try to sound like a woman of the world. Don't try to change yourself, heart of my heart. You delight me just as you are."

"I know why you feel guilty," she said, laughing. "It's because you made up that story to get me here."

"What story?" he said frowning.

"About Leonardo da Vinci and the man who was executed."

Valerio rose abruptly and left the room. He returned a moment later, carrying a large book. Seating himself beside her on the bed he flicked over the pages.

"There," he said at last, thrusting the book at her.

Helena looked at the page. It contained a reproduction of a pencil sketch of a man in long flowing robes, hanging from a rope around his neck. The caption identified him as Bernardo Baroncelli, depicted at his execution by Leonardo da Vinci.

"I'm sorry," she said, feeling foolish. "I should have known you wouldn't tell a lie—not with your oversize conscience."

He grimaced. "You have the power to make my conscience fall silent, heart of my heart. If poor old Baroncelli hadn't presented himself I should have had to think up some other way to get you into my arms. Because that's where I've been determined to have you since the first moment. It's where you belong—where you will always belong...."

Three

In later years Helena was always confused about what her real feelings for Valerio had been. Sometimes she felt she'd been wildly, passionately in love with him. At others she felt she was simply in love with the whole of life, and he was a part of it. In her eyes he was surrounded by a cloud of delight that enveloped everything. She was successful at the academy and good at her work. A brilliant future stretched before her, and she had Valerio to love. What could be more perfect?

She accepted their love as a child accepts the good things its parents provide, with confidence and ease and with no fear that they may not be there tomorrow. Her heart had never been broken and it seemed only natural that the man she wanted should want her.

Officially she continued to live at the hostel, but every spare moment was spent in Valerio's apartment. He would leave her alone to do her work, but often she would look up to find his eyes on her, and she would push the work aside and throw herself into his arms.

She loved Florence and her present life, but she also found her mind leaping ahead to the vast horizons that stretched out for her in the coming years. In her dreams she packed up her easel and paints and wandered to distant parts of the world seeking out the strange and exotic to capture on canvas. The fact that the dream allowed no place for Valerio was something that troubled her only slightly. That was the beauty of fantasies. One could afford to ignore the contradictions. She knew she couldn't bear to part with Valerio, but she also wanted her dream. The practical difficulties were something she'd sort out later.

She would talk about her ambitions to Valerio, and if he was a little quiet on those occasions she hardly noticed. When his silence did catch her attention she would kiss him until his face lightened, confident that she had dismissed the problem. And so she blundered on and never saw the danger.

She was intoxicated with the sensation of having divided into two people. The new Helena had a life of her own, and demands of her own that sometimes conflicted with what the old Helena wanted. The old one would be working away at a sketch, lost in the excitement of creation and fulfillment. But the new one would plead in urgent tones for the ecstasy of Valerio's arms and the different kind of fulfillment to be found there.

Her new self was alive to Valerio as a physical being every second of the day, no matter what else she might be doing. It was a self whose thoughts dwelt on the shape of his body, the set of his head, the graceful movements of his hands. It was a pagan, wanton self. When it took over she could sit and listen to his grave talk and take in nothing but the beauty of his mouth, the way his lips moved and how the light played on his high cheekbones.

Sometimes the two selves united, and the joy of her senses would be translated undimmed into paint on canvas. There was a new quality about her pictures then, a ravishing sensual glow that she never afterwards recaptured. At such times she felt the perfect harmony of her life as a tangible thing, with every separate part working toward a perfect whole.

But at other times the separate parts obstinately refused to meld together. They flew apart and waged a troublesome war within her, a war that carried the seeds of tragedy, if she hadn't been too lost in happiness to see it.

She was enchanted too by the change in Valerio when they were alone. His happiness transformed him into another man. He still smiled rarely, but when he did his smile was brilliant with joy, giving her the deep, feminine satisfaction of knowing that she had worked this miracle. In the company of others he was the old Valerio, grave and reserved, perhaps a little cold. Even then his hand would steal toward hers, but only under the table where no one could see. A public gesture of affection came very hard to him.

One Friday night in June she broke the hostel's rules and stayed away all night. When she woke the next morning the memory of the blissful hours she had spent in Valerio's arms was still with her, bathing her in happiness.

"I don't care if the dragon rages," she told him as she sat up in bed to take the coffee he'd brought her. "I don't care about anything. It was a perfect night, and now it's a perfect morning."

"It's not morning," he chided her. "It is midday, sleepy-head. If you don't get up at once we shall be too late for our picnic. Also," he added, raising one ironic eyebrow, "you had best cover yourself—otherwise I'll join you in bed and keep you there till tomorrow. Then you'll have another night to explain to the dragon."

She chuckled and hastened to get up. They left the apartment an hour later to drive into the Tuscan hills for their picnic. But as soon as they were in the street she heard Valerio draw in his breath sharply. Advancing toward them down the street was an elderly man, who stopped, hesitated, and for a moment Helena thought he would turn and cross the road to avoid them. But Valerio called to him and at once the man's face cleared. He came toward them with his hand stretched out and a smile of greeting on his face.

"Signor Corelli, I would like you to meet Signorina James," said Valerio in his most formal voice. He went on to introduce the old man to Helena, and when she heard his full name she recognized him as one of the most eminent judges in Florence. Valerio had spoken of him as a friend of his late father.

They exchanged civilities for a few minutes, then Signor Corelli bade them farewell. He had been speaking perfect Italian, but at the last moment he switched to the Tuscan dialect to say, "Well done, my boy. It's about time."

Then he clapped Valerio on the shoulder and gave Helena a beaming smile that did not hide the fact that he was examining her keenly, and hurried off. She stared after him. "What did he mean? About time for what?"

Valerio had grown slightly red. "About time I was married," he said. "He thinks we are engaged."

"But why? Did you tell him we were?"

"In a sense. It was obvious to him that you had stayed the night in my home, and I introduced you to him. To a man of his generation that would be conclusive. Did you see how he hesitated when he first saw us?"

"Yes. I thought he was going to cross the street."

"He would have if I'd given him no sign. He's nearly eighty. In his youth there were two kinds of woman, and he has never forgotten it. He would have concluded that you were my 'little friend,' and he would have held you cheap. I won't allow anyone to think that of you."

"It was nice of you to think of my reputation," she said, touched by this old-fashioned gallantry. "But haven't you damaged your own reputation, with him? Sooner or later he's going to discover the truth."

"What truth?"

"That we're not engaged."

They were walking along the street by this time, so he was able to avoid looking at her as he said, "Are you never going to marry me, my Helena?"

"Not just because you've 'compromised' me," she said promptly. "Or rather not because we've compromised each other. Honestly darling, how can you be so nineteenth century? You don't have to make an honest woman of me."

"Don't ever say such a thing again!" he said, turning on her so fiercely that several passersby stared at them.

She was momentarily diverted by the fact that Valerio had actually displayed violent emotion in a public place, something unthinkable with him. But then she saw the genuine anger in his eyes and her laughter faded. Valerio had recovered himself a little.

"We can't discuss this here," he said firmly and took her by the arm to lead her to where his car was parked. He drove faster than usual till they had reached the place in the hills where they were to have the picnic. When they got out he chose a spot well shaded by trees. He made no further mention of the subject till they had unpacked the picnic things and were sitting down.

"I wonder if you know what pain it gives me when you make such jokes," he said quietly. "It makes cheap something that is sacred to me. In my eyes you are already my wife and above all other women. To speak of my making an honest woman of you is—" he hunted around for the worst condemnation he could find "—it is vulgar."

"I'm sorry," she said at once, perceiving that he was really offended. "I only meant that I didn't want you to feel that you *had* to marry me. That's not the right reason."

"And what is the right reason?"

"That you love me."

"Do you doubt that I love you, Helena, even though I haven't said so?"

She shook her head.

"And you?" he went on. "Does the idea of our marriage dismay you? Have you no love for me?"

"I do love you," she said earnestly. "I'm just not sure that I want to get married *now*. I hadn't thought I'd get married for years."

"I know," he said in a brooding voice. "I come second to your hitchhike round the world, don't I?"

"Not second," she assured him. "But I want that trip as well. I want to work and travel and find out who I am and what I can do."

"You are my love, and you can make me happy," he said at once.

She said nothing. His words had laid the problem before her in stark terms. For a woman of another generation to be a man's love and able to make him happy would have been enough. But Helena wanted more, and she couldn't bear to hurt Valerio further by telling him that his love wasn't enough for her.

Fortunately he saved her from having to do so. While she was still floundering for words he changed the subject. For the rest of the picnic they discussed indifferent matters, but for both of them it was an effort.

They returned to his apartment in the evening, and heard the telephone ringing as soon as they got in. Valerio snatched it up and said "Mama!"

After a moment he looked at Helena and said "Wednesday!" and raised an eyebrow to her. She nodded. There was nothing else to do.

"That was to be expected," Valerio said when he had put the phone down. "Signor Corelli is a great man but he is also the biggest gossip in Florence. He was on the telephone to my mother within ten minutes and now she wants to meet you. She would be so hurt if I didn't take you to meet her. She was a little offended that I hadn't already done so."

The following Wednesday evening Helena put on a demure long dress and allowed Valerio to drive her to his family home on the edge of the city. It had belonged to his father. Now it was Valerio's property, although his mother still lived there, so Helena regarded it with special interest, as she knew that Valerio considered it her future home. Whether she thought so herself was something she hadn't fully decided.

The Villa Lucci was on a hill to the north of the city. The land was so steep the the gardens surrounding the building were laid out in tiers. Even on the ground floor Helena could look out on all Florence below her, bathed in the light of the setting sun.

The house was very old and rather dark. To Helena, who liked a light atmosphere, it seemed gloomy. But she was entranced by the multitude of paintings that Valerio told her had been collected by his father.

From the first moment she knew she was under inspection from three pairs of avidly curious eyes. Valerio's mother, his grandmother and his young sister all regarded her with a keenness that betrayed their thoughts.

Despite the uncomfortable feeling this gave her, Helena kept her head up, assisted by the tender protectiveness with which Valerio surrounded her. It was obvious that he'd made his intentions plain to his family, and insisted that she be welcomed. The Signora Lucci showed her a gracious courtesy that became warmer as the evening wore on. Helena had the feeling that she'd passed a test.

Valerio's grandmother was a large, jovial lady who welcomed her with a beaming smile and a kiss on both cheeks. She insisted that Helena should call her Adele, which obviously pleased Valerio. Serena was a well-behaved child, shy and stiff at first, but melting later. If her eager questions were anything to go by she too had taken to her future sister-in-law.

When the dinner was over, the *signora* took Helena aside and encouraged her to talk about herself. By this time Helena had relaxed, and she talked more freely than she might otherwise have done about her passion for painting. Valerio's mother listened to these disclosures with a gracious smile.

"How much you remind me of myself at your age," she said at last. "I too studied art. It was eventually a great help to me because my husband was a connoisseur, and it is so important that a woman should be able to discuss her husband's interests, is it not?"

Helena stiffened. "I'm studying at the academy for my own sake," she said firmly. "I've always wanted to be a painter."

"How wise of you to have an ambition," said the *signora* with a smile. "In my day we sat about waiting to get married...."

Adele, who had joined them, gave a laugh that was almost a cackle. "Speak for yourself," she declared. "I didn't sit about waiting."

Helena joined in the old woman's laughter. She liked Adele a great deal. The *signora* sat impassive, her faint smile riveted onto her face, until the other two had finished. Evidently she was not amused by this outspoken humor, but she was too well-bred to say so.

"My mother-in-law does not come from Florence," she said at last, "but from Rome. It was on a journey to this city that she met my father-in-law. In that respect she is like yourself, *signorina*. If you had not come to the Florence academy you would not have met my son."

Plainly she considered Helena's artistic ambition as no more than the modern way of husband-hunting, and nothing was going to convince her otherwise. Helena turned the conversation into what she hoped were safer channels.

"Well, Valerio told me once that I reminded him of his grandmother," she said.

"I can imagine," said the *signora*, and Helena had the feeling that she had gone down several notches in her estimation.

When it was time to leave, Adele clasped Helena to her capacious bosom and gave her a warm kiss.

"For too long this house has been dark and gloomy," she said. "You will fill it with children and I shall see them before I die."

On the way home Helena repeated this to Valerio and said, "You ought to have made it more plain to them that this is going to be a long engagement."

"I tried to, but I don't think it sank in. Besides, how long?"

"We've been through all this. I want to finish at the academy and then see some of the world before I settle down."

"In short, you want me to wait several years," he said bitterly, and that night they had the nearest thing they had ever had to a quarrel.

At the midterm break Valerio accompanied her to England to meet her father. Here at least she thought there would be a counsel of delay to back her up. But her father merely said, "You'll be eighteen in no time, and then you won't need my consent. Besides, he seems a decent chap, and at least you won't be poor."

In which Helena thought, accurately, she could detect the hand of her stepmother.

She returned to Florence in a state of utter confusion. She was in love and the man she loved wanted to marry her. But instead of being wildly happy she felt that a net was closing about her.

The life she would live as Valerio's wife was becoming increasingly clear. He wanted a summer wedding, and then she could return to the academy for her final year. He had agreed to that. But Helena knew that as soon as the wedding was over the pressure for her to have a child would begin, if not from him then from his family. And soon he too would begin to insist, for she knew that he longed for children.

She didn't want to lose Valerio, but neither did she want the life he was urging on her. She wanted to enjoy her youth and her work as well as her love. She wanted the freedom to be reckless and stupid and irresponsible. She wanted to stretch her talents to the utmost, and if a picture was going well she wanted to be able to shut out the world for days on end while she worked on it. And if that was selfish, then she wanted the right to be selfish.

What she was offered instead was a life of premature middle age in that gloomy villa on the hill. She would be the wife of a rising young lawyer and expected to behave as such. Her friends would cease to be the genial eccentrics she met at the academy, and in whose company she rejoiced. She would move instead among judges and sober-suited professional men, and other sedate Florentine matrons. And she would have to become one of them, or Valerio would suffer. It might sound old-fashioned, but Valerio was an old-fashioned man and he moved in an old-fashioned society.

Often she lay awake in the night, arguing the matter out, and at those times it seemed very simple. She must talk to Valerio and make him realize that she couldn't be rushed into their marriage. Occasionally she told herself that he would be secretly relieved. Whatever he might say, he had a guilty conscience about her, and it was only his strong sense of duty that was making him marry her.

But these arguments would fade in the dawn. When they met, for she saw him every day now, she would be flooded anew with the happiness of being with him. And when he looked at her with eyes softened by love, and called her "heart of my heart" in the tender voice that he used only for her, she knew very well that his reason for this marriage wasn't guilt.

Then it was her turn to feel guilty, for this wonderful, passionately loving man was offering her the gift of himself, wholly open and trusting, with nothing held back—and it wasn't enough for her.

The wedding date was set for August when the academy year was over, giving them time for their honeymoon before the following term. Helena, conscious of Valerio's diamond ring weighing down her left hand, had tried once more to make him understand her apprehension. He had listened to her with a tender, understanding smile on his face that had told her he was simply waiting for her to finish, before soothing what he plainly took to be a case of prewedding nerves.

"Are you telling me that you no longer love me?" he asked at last. "Or that you never did?"

"You know I love you. I'm just happy the way we are. Can't we go on this way for a while yet?"

"It's gone too far, darling. We're already 'official.' It's too late to go back on that. And if you plan to marry me in the end, why not now? I'm not a monster, am I?"

She'd answered that by kissing him and at once his arms had gone around her, pulling her down onto the bed beside him. He'd made love to her as never before, fiercely demanding but also giving, taking her to a pitch of ecstasy that left her exhausted, shaking and incapable of thought.

She clung to him, knowing that she belonged to this man because no other would ever ignite in her such passion. Drained and blissful, she found that her fears had receded into the far distance. It never occurred to her that behind the gentleness of his ways Valerio could be as ruthless as any other man when something threatened his possession of the woman he loved.

But her mood of contentment didn't last. It began to evaporate as soon as they were apart, to be replaced by a grim fear.

She felt that she was suffocating. If she went ahead with this marriage she would be swallowed up and vanish. As the days passed the fear grew until it verged on panic. Several times she woke in the night struggling for breath.

On the day of their marriage she woke to the knowledge that there was no way she could go through with it. She quailed when she thought of what she was doing, but she knew she had no choice. She felt as though she was fighting for her life.

Her father and stepmother had arrived in Florence two days earlier and Helena had joined them in their hotel. On her wedding morning, as Helena argued back and forth with herself, trying to pluck up courage for the step she must take, her stepmother fussed around her to get her ready. By the time Helena had got up her nerve, she was dressed in full bridal apparel.

She took an anguished look at herself in the full-length mirror. She was a beautiful bride, and she knew how Valerio's eyes would have radiated joy at the sight of her. For a moment she wavered. It would be so easy to go through with it, to continue being carried along by the tide that had carried her this far.

Then her resolve stiffened and she turned her back on that enticing figure in the mirror. With shaking fingers she dialed Valerio's number, and felt a stab of misery at the sound of his voice, full of gladness when he heard her. She could hardly stammer out the words she had to say. "Please, Valerio, I've got to talk to you, explain why I can't do it—"

"Darling, I can't hear what you're saying. Your voice sounds strange. Are you crying?"

"Yes," she said desperately, wiping away the tears. "I can't marry you—not today—please try to understand. I know it's the last minute—but I *can't....*"

The last word came out as a hoarse whisper. She sat there trembling, trying to prevent a rising tide of hysteria from engulfing her.

"Darling, listen to me." Valerio's voice sounded firm, and had a no-nonsense tone that he'd never used with her before. "You have to stop this. Of course you've got nerves. I'm scared myself. But we love each other, you must hang on to that."

"I do love you, but I'm not ready to marry you—"

"It's too late to say that. You have promised me, and in an hour we will meet in the church."

"No!" she cried. "I won't be there. You have to believe me. Please, Valerio, don't go to the church. *I won't be there!"*

"I don't believe that. I know how today has frightened you, but when it's over you will feel better. We've talked of this before and you've always been sensible in the end. Please, my heart, don't be silly now—"

"You don't understand," she choked. "I've tried to make you understand, but you never have. I'm sorry, Valerio, but I won't be there. You mustn't go..."

"Listen to me, darling." Valerio's voice was gentle but still firm. "I am going to the church now—and so are you. I know this will pass soon. You are too strong and good to do this to me because of a foolish fancy. Goodbye, my love."

She had sat staring blankly at the phone, which went dead. Something was choking her. She could no longer fight down the hysteria. She tore off her headdress. Then she pulled open the door and fled down the stairs into the street.

She didn't see where she ran, nor did she look at the time. Later her father told her that she'd been missing for three hours when he found her wandering by the river, oblivious to the curious stares drawn by her tearstained face and her disheveled wedding dress.

Valerio had gone to the church, said her father, and waited for her till he was finally convinced that she wasn't coming. After an hour he had left with a look on his face that was "unlike anything I've ever seen on any man's before."

She returned to the hotel and changed out of her bridal dress. Now that her decision was irrevocable she felt oddly calmer and strong enough for the ordeal that faced her. She was going to Valerio's apartment to plead for his understanding and forgiveness. He loved her. Surely that would be stronger in him than his pain and anger? Surely he would remember that she'd tried to warn him? In a recklessly optimistic moment she even dared to hope that he would agree to put the clock back and let things be as they were before.

She found Valerio's door locked against her. Her frantic knocking and pleading produced no sign of response. At last she went away. She wrote him a long, desperate letter, full of her love and longing for his forgiveness. After a silence lasting many weeks the letter was returned to her, unopened.

That was her last contact with him. For ten years she neither saw nor heard from Valerio Lucci, until the day he walked into her room at the Heart of Mercy Hospital.

Four

Helena's mind was whirling, refusing to take in what had happened. This man who hated her now held her future in his hands. In the long, frozen moment while she looked at him, every detail of Valerio Lucci was imprinted on her brain.

He had altered. He was tall, and his build had sometimes seemed too slight for his inches, but the years had given him the extra weight needed to make him impressive. He carried no surplus flesh, but his shoulders had broadened and every line of his body now suggested power.

It was his face that held her. It bore harsh lines that she hadn't seen before. His eyes seemed darker than ever, and more shadowed, but his mouth had changes the most. Where once it had been merely resolute, now it bore signs of hardness. And yet, to her eyes it hadn't changed at all. It was still the strong, beautiful mouth that had once kissed her with such joy and tenderness.

How could he sit there so coolly, taking papers from his briefcase, speaking of their tragedy in that ironic voice, as though it had happened to someone else?

"I would like you to tell me everything that you can remember," he said now. "I understand that your memory has gaps, but you must do the best you can."

"Valerio—"

He raised his head to look at her, and spoke dispassionately. *"Signora*, it is better if we understand each other from the outset. I am a professional man, who has been employed to do a job for someone who needs my sevices. I was informed that the name of my client was Signora Catesby, nothing more.

"Now that I am here, and discover that you are someone with whom I was once acquainted, it makes no difference. The relationship between us is quite impersonal. Between client and lawyer there can be nothing else, as I am sure you appreciate. Is that not so, *signora*?"

He said the last word with quiet but clear emphasis, and she understood. Perhaps, she thought, it was better this way. Valerio's professional detachment was her only hope.

"Of course," she said, "Signor Lucci."

He nodded as though he was satisfied, and returned to studying the papers. "I have here a copy of the statement that you gave the police. It's unfortunate that you can't remember more than this. Or perhaps something has come back to you in the meantime?"

"Nothing," she said hopelessly. "I have to accept that I was driving that car, but I don't know why. I've always hated driving on the Continent. It confuses me and I've never really got the hang of it."

She wanted to say "Surely you remember that?" but after his earlier prohibition she didn't dare. But then she knew it was unnecessary, for a stillness had come over him. He wasn't looking at her, but from the angle of his averted face and the set of his shoulders she knew that he too was remembering the day when he had let her drive his car in a country lane, and she'd become hopelessly muddled by the unfamiliar steering, and taken them into a ditch.

Luckily they had had the road to themselves, and no one was hurt, but he had to hire a tractor to rescue his car. Helena recalled, as if it was yesterday, the walk back to Florence, his arm around her shoulder, and his voice firm and loving, saying, "That is positively the last time. You are too precious to risk, heart of my heart."

After a moment Valerio came to life again. He reached into his briefcase and took out a small leather pouch. From it he took a pair of black-rimmed glasses and put them on. She had the feeling that he had donned a visor, and his face was now guarded from her more than ever.

"How much did you have to drink?" he asked.

"I don't know," she said desperately. "It must have been quite a lot, but I don't recall anything after we got to the party."

"We? Oh, yes, you were with a Mr. Brian Hanley, were you not? Tell me about him."

"He's my employer. I work for Hanley Leather Goods as his designer. We came to Florence for the Design Fair. The party was given by someone he met at the fair. We went in a rented car, and he drove us there. But on the way back I apparently insisted on driving."

Valerio looked up at her sharply. "What do you mean 'apparently'?"

"I don't remember it, but it's what Brian says I did."

"To whom has he said this?"

"To me."

"You mean the police have allowed you to see him?"

"No, he wasn't supposed to, but he was worried about me. He came to make sure I was all right. He even tried to stay here when the policeman came in, but the sister wouldn't let him."

"Do you mean that he saw you before the police did?"

"Yes."

"And afterward?"

"No, he's been kept out ever since. But why does it matter?"

"Do the police know that he saw you?"

"I don't think so. But what difference does it make?"

"Possibly none, but it is as well that he wasn't caught. It smacks of collaboration and would make them suspicious."

"Well I've told the police all I know now, so it can't make any difference if I see Brian. Can you make them let him in?"

"I won't even try. I want you to see as little of him as possible."

"But *why*?"

He regarded her sternly. "Because your interests aren't necessarily the same as his. He too may be facing charges."

"How can he possibly be? I was driving the car."

"Just the same, if you don't remember what happened I don't want him confusing you with his version."

"That's an outrageous thing to say," she said hotly. "Brian's the most decent, kindly man who ever lived."

"Possibly," said Valerio dryly. "But I see from the papers that he's a member of Parliament. If he has any instinct for survival at all—and he could hardly be an M.P. without one—then he's bound to present his story in the way that will be most favorable to himself. And what is favorable to him, may not be for you."

"If you mean that he'd tell lies about me to save himself, I don't believe it. He loves me. He wants to marry me. He'd never do a deceitful thing like that." The warmth of Brian's loyalty was still with her, and indignation at hearing him slandered made her speak impulsively. Only when the words were out did she realize how they must sound to this man, who had once so nearly become her husband.

But Valerio gave no sign that her angry assertion meant anything to him. He was studying the papers again. "I didn't realize that you were engaged to be married," he said, his voice emotionless. "In that case, of course, you obviously know him very well, and perhaps your view of him is correct."

"I didn't say we were engaged," Helena said wearily. "I just said he'd asked me. But I'm probably going to jail...." Her voice shook on the word *jail*, and she fought to keep her composure. It would never do to break down again in front of Valerio.

"I should prefer you not to talk like that," said Valerio firmly. "It's my job to keep you out of jail, and I don't despair of doing so."

"But what kind of chance do I have?" she said desperately. "Is it really true that I could be sentenced for as long as ten years?"

"That is most unlikely—"

"But is it possible? I have to know."

Valerio hesitated, and for the first time since he had entered the room his voice was gentle.

"Very well, it is possible. *If* Lucilla Dorani dies, and *if* they can prove that you were driving under the influence of alcohol, then the sentence might be ten years. But it is by no means certain that these things will happen." For a brief moment he reached out and laid his hand lightly over hers. "You aren't alone now, don't forget that. I am here to fight for you, and I won't let you go to prison. I've had clients whose cases looked far blacker than yours, and they've walked away free."

His eyes held hers, seeming to hypnotize her into a state of calm. She felt herself relax as his quiet confidence began to pass from him to herself as though traveling through the touch of their flesh. After a moment he took his hand away. When he spoke again it was in the firm, impersonal voice he had used earlier.

"For the moment, I need to know how I can get hold of your driving license. At least we can show the court that you possess one, even if you didn't have it with you. How can I contact your husband?"

"I've no idea. I haven't seen him since our divorce two years ago. I live alone."

"Let me have your address, and tell me how I can get in."

She gave him the address and said, "I'll have to let you have the key. It's in my bag."

While she was rummaging for it he said, "Have you any previous driving convictions?"

"None at all."

"That's useful. It'll help at the preliminary hearing, which I am working to have brought forward to the earliest possible date. In this, I imagine, I shall have the assistance of Mr. Hanley's lawyer."

"But aren't you Mr. Hanley's lawyer?"

"No. I represent only you. I told you, your interests may conflict with his."

"I don't understand about the hearing. Surely the later it's held the more chance I have of remembering something?"

"Suppose you remember something damaging? Or suppose Lucilla Dorani recovers consciousness and says something that damns you? This is only a hearing, not a trial. I want your first appearance to be while there is as little evidence against you as possible."

"But what possible difference can that make?"

"You must take it from me that it will make a difference. You must try to trust me, *signora*—" for a moment the impassiveness of his face shifted slightly, and there was almost irony in his voice as he added "—although I appreciate that you may find that hard. Now, can we return to the matter in hand? The party—you have no recollections about it? That surprises me. I have heard Lorenzo Santi's parties spoken of as occasions that live in the memory forever. Was his current boyfriend there—or couldn't you tell him apart from the other girls?"

Helena flushed at the contempt in Valerio's voice, but in the same moment she realized that he had—whether by accident or design—given her memory a jolt. Vague images were flickering in her mind again, and she reached out urgent hands to grasp at them.

"I remember...feeling uncomfortable at being there," she said. "It wasn't the sort of scene I enjoy. I didn't belong...."

"Didn't you?" he said coolly. "Are you sure you had no idea in advance what kind of party you were going to?"

"No, I didn't," she said angrily. "And I don't see that that question has any relevance to my case."

Now it was his turn to flush. "It has none," he conceded after an awkward moment. "Please continue with your recollections."

"That's all. I don't remember leaving, or giving a lift to Lucilla. Brian says she was worried about not being able to get home. Her brother didn't know she was there."

"She has no brother," said Valerio.

"You know her?"

"Slightly. Her family is friendly with mine."

"The man she was worried about is called Guido. If he isn't her brother, who is he?"

"Guido Ranelli is her fiancé. He would certainly not have approved of her going to Santi's home. Was she alone?"

"She went with another man, who dumped her."

"So she was desperate to get home, and you and Mr. Hanley offered her a lift?"

"Yes, but now I'm telling you what Brian told me. I have no recollection of this myself."

"No matter. I shall leave things there for the moment. You must be tired." Valerio had begun to get his things together. His long fingers made swift, nervous movements, and he didn't look at her as he added, "Do you have any family at all that I should contact...any children?"

"I have no children," she said in a voice as carefully toneless as his. "My father is dead and the only relatives I have are my stepmother and two half brothers under ten. I don't think you need trouble them."

"I will contact your stepmother and assure her of my best efforts on your behalf." Valerio removed his reading glasses and rose to go. "I hope that you too can bring yourself to accept that assurance, *signora*. Now I will leave you. Please try to get some rest. I will be in touch very soon."

He departed at once, without shaking her hand or showing any disposition to linger. Helena lay staring at the door, feeling as though she'd been twisted into knots and wrung out. Beneath the formality of their conversation she knew that both she and Valerio had exchanged a great deal of unspoken information.

He knew that her dreams had come to nothing. She'd finished up doing the kind of commercial designing on which she had once poured youthful scorn. After rejecting him she had married another man, and the marriage had failed.

Her knowledge of him was less specific, but equally telling. He'd made a success of his career. John Driffield had spoken of getting the best lawyer in Florence, and then had called Valerio Lucci. Everything about him radiated prosperity. It wasn't just that his clothes were of the finest quality, that his shirt was of Egyptian cotton, his tie was silk and his suit superbly tailored. It had more to do with the air of assurance that he carried like a badge of achievement. Her defection hadn't broken Valerio. She was the one who was broken.

She wondered whether he was married, and guessed that he was not. There was no wedding ring on his left hand, which might have meant nothing, but she remembered how he'd planned to wear one for their marriage, as Italian men often did. He had shown her how they would exchange rings during the church ceremony, and bent his head to kiss the third finger of her left hand.

Most of all, she knew that he wasn't as indifferent to their meeting as he pretended. There'd been two brief moments when he had been as rent apart by memory as herself. But his self-control had come to his rescue.

She wondered about the hardness she'd seen in the set of his mouth. How deep did it go, and how much of the blame for it should be set at her door?

The events of the past few hours had already left her nerves in a jangle. Now, added to that was the shock of meeting the man whose ghost had given her no peace for ten years.

It was useless to tell herself that after all this time the past was safely dead. Valerio had taught her love when the world was young and green. With him she had known the best of love, its sweetness and tenderness as well as its passion. He had been sometimes gentle, sometimes fierce and demanding, but never less than generous. She had understood this only years later when she had found herself married to a man whose selfishness infused every area of his life. Then it had only hurt to recall Valerio's tender consideration.

She'd told herself proudly that she would have no regrets. What she had done, she had done, and she would live with the consequences, making no complaint. But the man she had loved would not be so easily silenced. She'd walked away from him in her life, but she couldn't walk away from him in her heart. He followed her, quietly, insistently forcing her to measure every other man against him, until finally she understood her tragic mistake.

She refused to waste time in wishing the past undone. She was a different woman, and Valerio was a different man. And the people they had become had nothing in common with the boy and girl who'd once loved each other so passionately. Only the memories remained to connect them with that time, and memories were a weakness that she could overcome.

At least, so she had thought, until Valerio Lucci had walked into her room, and her heart had given a leap of senseless joy.

It was four days before anything happened. Then the sergeant visited her to tell her that there had been no change in the condition of Lucilla Dorani, and that the preliminary hearing had been set for the following day. Helena was out of bed by now and sitting by the window. The sergeant commented politely that he was glad to see that she had improved, but sorry that she was still bad enough to need a bandage around her head.

Helena made an indifferent reply, but was careful to say no more. The bandage had, in fact, been the subject of some dispute between her and the doctor. In her opinion the injury to her head was not so bad as to need it. A large sticking plaster would have done, or even nothing at all. But the doctor had remained adamant, and it finally occurred to her that perhaps he was kindly trying to delay the moment when she would be taken to prison.

But now she knew the moment could be delayed no longer. Once she'd appeared at the hearing she would be officially well enough to be removed from the hospital.

The sister who cared for her plainly thought so, too, for on the day of the hearing she told Helena to pack her suitcase. She watched intently as Helena got to work and at last she seized on a dark, plain dress and said, "You must wear this."

Obviously this was suitable court wear for a woman under arrest. Helena put on the dress without argument, although she thought it looked hideous without makeup in her present pallid condition. She tried to modify the effect by applying a little lipstick, but the sister restrained her. This time Helena attempted a protest, but the sister said firmly, "Those are my instructions."

It was in a mood of bleak depression that Helena got into the police car that came for her. Already she was being treated as though she was in jail, and by nightfall she probably would be.

At the courthouse she was handed into the care of a young policewoman who showed her into an anteroom and left her. Helena stared at herself in the small mirror on the wall. She had never looked worse in her life. She was still pale and washed out, and the bruise high on one cheekbone looked deep purple by contrast. The unadorned dark dress and white bandage completed the depressing effect.

Suddenly she rebelled. She might be a prisoner but she wasn't going to let them force her to look like one before it was necessary. She went through her handbag and hurriedly applied some lipstick. Then she took out some beige cream that she used for covering blemishes and rubbed it over her bruise. That was an improvement. If she took off the bandage, she decided, she would look quite human. Her hands were moving toward it when the door opened and a furious voice said, *"What the devil do you think you're doing?"*

In a moment Valerio was beside her, firmly pulling her hands away from her face.

"Let me go," she said furiously. "I'm not going in there looking like a walking corpse. Let me keep some self-respect!"

"Is your self-respect more important to you than your freedom?" he demanded, still holding her wrists. "I *want* you looking like a walking corpse. It may be your one hope today."

"But why? What difference can it make?"

"It may make all the difference to where you spend tonight. I haven't time to explain now. Clean that stuff off your face at once."

"But—"

"Do it, or I'll do it for you," he snapped. "I don't have time for the courtesies now. They'll be coming for you in a minute. I could wring your neck. That sister presented you exactly according to my instructions, and you try to ruin it."

"*Your* instructions?" She was rummaging in her bag as she spoke, trying to find some cleansing pads.

"Of course. I managed to get her on our side. I told her I wanted you looking thoroughly ill and frail. She knew what to do."

"And the bandage? Is the doctor taking your instructions too?"

"Florence is a very small society. You should know that. Your doctor and I play squash together every week. I merely hinted to him that it would be a pity to rush your recovery."

"It seems that everyone is in your confidence except me." She was looking into the mirror as she spoke and removing the makeup.

He turned on her suddenly. "Good God, Helena, what's happened to you? You used to be brighter than this! I want the court to feel some sympathy for you. I don't want you walking in there, made-up to the nines and looking healthy. That would merely make them contrast you with Lucilla Dorani, lying at death's door."

She stared at him. "I see. Yes, of course, I should have thought of that." She wondered if he knew that he'd called her Helena. He was again striding about the room, looking at his watch, glancing at the door, tense as a coiled spring.

"This is an Italian court," he went on with ironic emphasis. "A certain amount of melodrama is expected, I'm afraid. I've got to make them realize that you're a victim too; otherwise you'll find yourself cast in the role of attempted murderess."

"Melodrama? You?" she was surprised into saying.

He gave a smile which did not reach his eyes. "I am an Italian, Helena. I am as capable of donning the Punchinello mask for the sake of my client as any other Italian lawyer. No advocate who could not do so would last five minutes in this country."

"Can't you tell me what's going on?" she pleaded. "You're planning something, aren't you?"

"Naturally I am. Do you think I am so lacking in native cunning that I haven't worked out a few surprises for this situation? I'd be failing you if I hadn't. The facts are against you.

The atmosphere is against you. The people are against you. The only thing you have on your side is my ability to do a conjuring trick.''

It might have sounded conceited if he hadn't said it in such a clinical tone. This was a man who knew his own abilities, and was calmly dissecting them for her edification, without conceit, but without time-wasting false modesty either.

''I wish you'd tell me what to expect,'' she persisted.

''That would be fatal. I know your nature. It is open and candid...at least, about some things. You could never be as much of an actress as you'd need to be if you were warned beforehand. You must be taken totally by surprise.

''I'm sorry I couldn't give you my instructions personally about your appearance, but I only got back from England a couple of hours ago. I haven't been idle on your behalf. I called at the address you gave me and retrieved your license. I also managed to get some official documentation of your record as a driver, which luckily is spotless. It'll help, but not much. Here, let me look at you.''

He took her chin between his fingers and studied her face. She found it unnerving to be so close to him, subjected to that impersonal scrutiny. He took the little pad from her and wiped her cheek gently a few times.

''That'll have to do,'' he said at last. ''Now I want you to give me a promise. You'll do and say nothing except answer my questions, and any that the judge may ask you. And you'll agree to anything I say. *Whatever it is*, you'll just agree. Do I have your word?''

She stared at him wildly. In her present nervous state this blanket promise sounded ominous. It reminded her that behind his professional exterior Valerio had no reason to wish her well. He read her thoughts accurately, and a cold, ironic smile curled his lips. ''Sooner or later, *signora*,'' he said with soft, deadly intensity, ''you are going to have to decide whether or not you trust me.''

''Wouldn't it please you to see me in jail?'' she flung at him. ''Wouldn't you think I'd come by my just deserts?''

"If I was a vengeful man I would get all the satisfaction I need out of your present predicament. As it is, I don't think I have done anything to deserve the low opinion of me that you evidently have."

"I didn't say that."

"You didn't have to. It is plain that you are wondering if I intend to let your case go by default as a way of satisfying myself for your insult of ten years ago. But have I shown myself capable of such behavior? You betrayed me, not the other way around. I never played you false, Helena. Nor do I intend to start now. I cannot force you to believe that, but it is true."

"I do believe it," she said in a low voice. "I'm sorry I doubted you, Valerio, but I don't know why you're troubling about me at all."

"You're my client, and entitled to my best efforts."

"Is that all?" she couldn't resist asking.

He was silent for a moment. "No, it's not all," he said at last. "I don't wish to see you in prison, Helena. The past is gone, but not forgotten. You were dear to me once, and I will do my best for you in memory of that old love, just as I would lay flowers on your grave if you were dead.

"And if that doesn't convince you, then let me offer you a practical reason. The connection between us won't remain a secret for long. I'm a lawyer. I wouldn't want it said that I was once engaged to a woman who is serving a prison sentence."

"I wonder," she said sadly, "which of those two reasons is the more important one for you?"

He nodded. "I've wondered that myself. But it's a speculation that gets us nowhere. Now, if you are ready to go, I think it is time."

Five

Helena had once before been inside an Italian court, when Valerio had allowed her to watch him at work. She remembered how impressive it had been with the three black-robed judges sitting on a raised dais, and Valerio, also in a black robe, looking dignified and handsome.

To her relief, the court she was now taken to was much smaller and not so overpowering. This was an informal hearing, roughly corresponding to a magistrate's court in England, and there was only one judge. He sat up high, looking down on the thirty other people who crowded the chairs in the well of the court.

There was no dock. The accused had a chair just below the judge's dais, close to the table where the defence advocate sat.

As soon as Helena was taken into the court she stiffened with shock, for the first sight that met her eyes was Adele, Valerio's grandmother. The old woman had changed less than had her grandson. She was still sturdy and bright-eyed, and she looked keenly at Helena.

There was one other face there that caught her attention. It belonged to a man of about thirty, with deep-set eyes and a fierce expression. He turned on Helena a look of such intense hatred that she was astounded, for she couldn't remember ever having seen him before.

Valerio led her to the chair in the center of the court, just below the judge. Before seating herself she managed to take a quick look around. She caught Valerio's eyes on her, and wondered if he had guessed that she was looking for Brian, disappointed not to see him.

Obeying Valerio's instructions she remained quiet during the recital of the charges—driving without a license, and driving under the influence of alcohol. Advocate Ferone, acting for the prosecution, announced that he was not moving for an immediate trial as there was more evidence that needed to be collected for possible further charges. He asked that the prisoner should be held in custody for the moment. He opposed provisional liberty on the grounds that the prisoner would attempt to leave the country.

Then Valerio rose. "May I draw the court's attention to the length of time that is likely to pass before this matter comes to trial?" he said. "If time is allowed for the collection of evidence on 'possible further charges' it could be as long as a year. In the meantime, two charges have been put forward today.

"The first accuses my client of driving while not in possession of a valid license. In fact, Signora Catesby has a license, although it was not on her person at the time of the accident. I present it to the court, and draw attention to the fact that Signora Catesby's previous record as a driver is unblemished. In the eleven years since she first learned to drive, she has not so much as a parking conviction against her. I have a statement from the British authorities to that effect."

The judge looked at the license that Valerio handed him, then at the statement, and nodded.

"Very well. But I must remind you that this is the lesser charge, Advocate Lucci. The charge of driving under the influence of alcohol is far more serious."

"I agree, your honor. But may I point out that my client is unlikely to be found guilty on this count, as there is no evidence against her?"

There was a loud murmur in the court, and the judge gave Valerio a look of surprise.

"I repeat, there is no evidence," said Valerio firmly. "Only three people can know the facts. Of these, one is in a coma, one has no memory of the events and one is not present. I believe the court would need substantially more than this before it would be prepared to remand my client in custody."

"Who is this third witness?" demanded the judge of Advocate Ferone. "And why isn't he here?"

"Signor Hanley has not yet arrived," said Ferone, looking a little harassed. He was a middle-aged, bullnecked man, with a weary appearance. "I believe he may have mistaken the time. I've sent someone to his hotel to fetch him. When he arrives, he will confirm that the prisoner was drinking heavily immediately prior to getting into the car.

"I should also add that the prosecution is not inclined to take seriously the prisoner's claim that she remembers nothing. Our belief is that she has sought an easy refuge from having to reveal facts damaging to herself."

There was another murmur. Helena opened her mouth to protest but Valerio quelled her with a look of iron. She sank back into her chair, from which she had half risen, and fixed her eyes on him. He held her gaze for a moment, until he was sure he had controlled her, then he turned back to the judge. Her heart was thumping wildly. Everything now depended on Valerio. Then, to her horrified disbelief, she heard him say, "The defense also concedes that Signora Catesby may know more than she reveals."

"No!"

Helena's wild scream rang through the court. There was noisy commotion. The judge banged his gavel. Under cover of the din Valerio dropped to his knees beside Helena. His eyes blazed fiercely into hers.

"You promised to trust me!" he hissed. *"If you break your word now I can do nothing for you!"*

She stared at him, dumb with despair. His eyes seemed to hypnotize her, promising her safety. Gradually her hands unclenched and she managed to nod.

As the hubbub died down she found herself looking at the unknown man whose glance of hatred had startled her when she first came into court. His face now was even more unnerving. He was taking a wolfish pleasure in her agony and making no attempt to hide it.

"I should like to question my client," said Valerio. "*Signora*, will you tell the court how you came to be in Florence?"

Helena pulled herself together. She had promised Valerio that she would put herself in his hands, and she had no choice but to do so. Trying to keep her voice firm, she gave a brief history of her employment with Hanley Leather Goods. Valerio nodded.

"Now," he said, "I should like you to recall the first conversation between us in the Heart of Mercy Hospital. Please repeat to the court the words you said to me on that occasion about Signor Hanley."

She frowned, not certain that she had understood him correctly.

"I am talking about the 'character reference' that you gave Signor Hanley, after I had expressed concern over the fact that he spoke to you before the police did," went on Valerio imperturbably.

This time the commotion was noisier than ever. Valerio quelled it by raising his voice and saying firmly, "I am asking the court to rule that nothing in Signora Catesby's statement to the police is allowable, because it was made after certain ideas had been planted in her head by Signor Hanley."

"What ideas?" demanded the judge gravely.

"I mean the idea that she had been drinking to excess. I mean the idea that she insisted on driving the car. Signora Catesby has no recollection of either of these things. Left to herself she would have vehemently denied them. But she as good as conceded both points in her statement, because she had been told they were true by someone she trusted."

The judge studied the papers on the desk before him.

"Was the prosecution aware of this?" he said sternly.

Advocate Ferone leaped to his feet. "The prosecution was not aware of any influence being exercised over the accused," he snapped. "Furthermore, the prosecution disputes that this meeting ever took place."

"Well, we will be able to question Signor Hanley on this matter—when he is good enough to arrive," said Valerio with a cold smile. He turned back to Helena. "Now, *signora*, my original question. Will you repeat to the court your description of Signor Hanley when we first spoke of him. Is it not true that you described him to me as 'the most decent, kindly man who ever lived'?"

"Yes, I did," she said, her voice tinged with anger. "And I also said that he'd never tell lies about me to save himself. You've no right to try to blacken him!"

Valerio ignored this last remark.

"Did you not also tell me," he went on, "that he was in love with you, and had asked you to marry him?"

She flushed. "Yes!" she said angrily.

She looked up at the judge, wondering why he permitted this. A compassionate man, he recognized the question in her eyes and said kindly, "This is not England, *signora*. The laws of evidence are somewhat more elastic here than in your country. Although I confess—" his glance moved to Valerio "—I should be glad to understand the purpose of these questions."

"The purpose is to make it clear that Signora Catesby is under a tragic delusion," said Valerio smoothly. "I believe that my client only took the wheel of that car as a way of preventing an accident—because the person who had been drinking to excess *was not herself but Brian Hanley*."

"This is outrageous!" Advocate Ferone jumped up again. "There is not the slightest evidence to sustain such an accusation. Advocate Lucci is merely throwing mud to blacken the name of an innocent man. These are the tactics of desperation."

The judge looked gravely at Valerio. "Certainly I should be sorry to think that this accusation had been made with no evidence whatever to back it up," he said.

"I wish to present these to the court," said Valerio, pulling some papers out of his briefcase. "They are copies of pages from an English newspaper. One is dated ten years ago, and reports the conviction of Brian Hanley on a charge of drunken driving. The other is dated eight years ago, and reports a second conviction on the same charge."

Helena sat up in her chair as though electrified. She had known nothing about either of these convictions, and she could clearly remember Brian having once laughingly told her that he'd never been in trouble with the law.

"On both occasions," Valerio continued, "there was nobody hurt, which doubtless accounts for the fact that these incidents rated only brief mentions in the local papers. But, as you will see, one report mentions Signor Hanley as having had six times the legal limit. It was only by the grace of God that he didn't kill someone."

"I protest!" Advocate Ferone shouted. "This is irrelevant to the present issue!"

"It does not relate directly," the judge agreed. "On the other hand, the court is entitled to take into account past conduct. Signora Catesby's previous unblemished record as a driver has been accepted as evidence." The judge turned and spoke to Helena. "*Signora*, did you know anything about these convictions?"

She shook her head. "I had no idea."

"Are you quite certain? If you are engaged to Signor Hanley, has he not confided any details of his past life to you? This is not the moment to be protecting him."

"I'm not protecting him," said Helena. "I knew nothing about this."

"And what about Advocate Lucci's theory that you were the driver because Signor Hanley was not sober? Do you have anything to say to that?"

"I don't remember," she insisted. "I really don't. That part of the evening is a total blank. Bri—Signor Hanley told me I'd insisted on driving, and I accepted it, because I was driving when the accident happened."

"But if you had only taken over driving in order to prevent an accident," persisted the judge, "it would certainly improve your position in the eyes of this court."

Now she understood why Valerio had suggested that she was concealing something. He'd been planning ahead for this moment, offering her a way out. But she couldn't take it. For a long moment she sat with her hand over her eyes.

"It's no use," she said at last in despair. "I can't remember anything."

She felt the pressure of Valerio's hand on her shoulder, and looked up, expecting to meet his anger because she had failed to take the escape he had offered her. Instead he was giving her a satisfied smile, as though she'd said something that pleased him. But she couldn't think what it was.

At that moment there was a noise from the back of the court, and a young, distracted-looking policeman hurried in. He went straight up to Advocate Ferone and muttered something in his ear. Helena saw the advocate turn white.

"What has happened?" demanded the judge.

Advocate Ferone rose to his feet. He looked as though all the stuffing had been knocked out of him. "It is with regret that I have to inform the court," he said, "that the prosecution will be unable to produce Signor Hanley at this hearing. I understand that he checked out of his hotel yesterday afternoon, and his whereabouts are unknown."

Valerio looked round the court. His face was brilliant, like a star actor who knows his moment has come. And an actor's sense of timing infused the delivery of his next words. "There is no difficulty about that," he said. "I can inform the court that Brian Hanley landed at London Airport yesterday evening. The prosecution's star witness has skipped town!"

The room was in an uproar. The judge banged his gavel uselessly and Valerio stood smiling at the commotion he had created. Helena hardly took in the implications of Brian's departure. She was fascinated by the sight of Valerio as she had never seen him before. Now she knew what he had meant by the Punchinello mask. Whatever his private reserve, in these impersonal surroundings his manner developed a touch of flamboyance, even—it was incredible, but true—of raffishness. He was at home in the spotlight, enjoying his own ability to dominate the seething court, which had responded so satisfactorily to the bombshell he had tossed into its midst.

He waited till the tumult had lasted long enough for his purposes, then he raised his voice and quelled the commotion as the judge's gavel had been unable to do.

"Brian Hanley has fled to England to save his own skin," he said in a voice full of contempt.

"That is impossible," howled Ferone. "The police still have his passport."

"That means nothing," said Valerio coolly. "A foreigner can leave this country without a passport if he's determined. And a British member of Parliament wouldn't have much trouble gaining admission to Britain, even without one." He turned and addressed the judge directly.

"I was in England myself yesterday, your honor, having gone there to obtain evidence of Hanley's previous convictions. I can further inform the court that the first thing Hanley did was to issue a statement through his lawyers for publication in the English press this morning. I managed to obtain a copy before I left."

He reached into his briefcase and took out another paper. "As it is in English," he said, "I will, with the court's permission, translate it aloud." Helena clenched her hands as Valerio began to read.

"It has been suggested to me that I issue a statement, following an incident in Italy where an employee of mine was involved in a road accident. The facts are these:

"Mrs. Helena Catesby, who is a designer employed by a leather-goods firm of which I am the owner, suggested to me that the two of us should attend the Design Fair in Florence. On the last evening of the fair we attended a reception at the home of Lorenzo Santi, a business contact that we had met there.

"I spent most of the evening discussing business with Signor Santi—" a burst of hastily suppressed laughter from the back of the court made Valerio pause before going on "—and saw very little of Mrs. Catesby. I do not know how much she had to drink. When we left she insisted on driving. There was nothing in her manner to make me think she was incapable, so I agreed. She assured me that she had a license in her possession.

"The front passenger seat was occupied by Signora Dorani, a young girl who had asked us to give her a lift home. I sat in the back. When the truck came into sight Mrs. Catesby appeared to lose her head, and swung straight into its path.

"Mrs. Catesby has always been an excellent employee, who has never previously been in trouble with the law. There is not, nor has there ever been, any personal relationship between Mrs. Catesby and myself."

There was silence as Valerio lowered the paper. Every eye in the courtroom was on Helena, who sat with her head bowed, her eyes fixed on the floor. She was stunned and sickened by Brian's treachery.

Then the silence was broken by a man's voice screaming, *"Serve you right, you drunken, murdering—"*

The crash of the judge's gavel silenced the rest. Helena's head jerked up and she saw that the outburst had come from the unknown man, who had been glaring at her. He was on his feet being restrained by a policeman. The judge's gavel smashed down again and again until there was silence.

"That is enough!" he snapped. "Signor Ranelli, I have every sympathy with your grief, but I will not tolerate such outbursts. If you cannot behave properly you will leave the court."

So that was it. This was Guido Ranelli, Lucilla's fiancé, and obviously he held Helena responsible for the girl's state. Helena was past blaming him. She wished drearily that they'd get the business over with and remove her somewhere out of the public eye.

Advocate Ferone was trying to make up lost ground. "Signor Hanley states clearly that the prisoner was in the driver's seat. She herself does not deny it. Furthermore he also states that she swung wildly into the path of the truck—"

"But the charge I have written down here says 'drunken driving,'" said the judge mildly. "Nothing in this statement supports that charge. Signor Hanley expressly says that he did not observe how much alcohol Signora Catesby consumed, and that she seemed fit to drive. She herself cannot remember how much—and I am bound to say that after what has occurred to-day I find her protestations of amnesia rather more convincing than you do—and Lucilla Dorani cannot tell us."

"There will be further charges of reckless driving—"

"Are you prepared to make and substantiate such charges now?" demanded the judge.

"Not at this moment." Ferone fumed.

"Then they cannot be the concern of this hearing. What is more, the testimony of a man who has—as Advocate Lucci so graphically puts it—'skipped town' is less than convincing."

"The prosecution asks that the prisoner should not be released at this moment," persisted Ferone. "Lucilla Dorani may recover consciousness at any time and give a statement confirming that the prisoner was driving dangerously. If the prisoner is allowed to leave the country in the meantime—"

Valerio rose again to his feet. "My client has no intention of leaving the country," he said. "She too is anxious to get the matter cleared up, confident that any further revelations will demonstrate her innocence. But to incarcerate her for anything up to a year on the kind of flimsy evidence that we have heard today, to imprison her to await trial on charges that may eventually have to be withdrawn, this is not justice.

"Advocate Ferone has made great play of my client's foreign nationality, and his fear that she may escape. But how can she escape? It is inconceivable that the police will be so careless a second time."

There was a rumble of laughter from the back of the court, and even the judge's face shifted slightly, as though he was trying to hold something in check.

"I should like to emphasize another aspect of my client's foreign status," Valerio continued. "She is alone and friendless in this country. Prison, for her, would be a far worse experience than for someone who had friends and relatives here.

"Signora Catesby has no living relatives who are prepared to help her. Her nearest kin is a stepmother, whom I visited while I was in England. I assured her of my best efforts for her step-daughter. Her response was to say she hoped it was clearly understood that she could not be responsible for my bill.''

There was a faint rumble from the body of the court. It was so quiet that Helena barely heard it, and yet she detected in it a hint of indignation, and an almost incredible message of hope. She held her breath, hardly daring to believe that Valerio was actually swinging the court's sympathy around to her.

"I assured her," Valerio went on dryly, "that I would expect nothing from her. Signora Catesby's ex-husband has not been in touch with her for two years. And now the one man she trusted, whom she believed she could rely on to support her in adversity, has cravenly escaped, leaving her to face everything alone. Finally, I ask the court to consider my client's state of health, which is still poor."

Helena saw the judge looking down at her with dark, compassionate eyes. He would see more than the bandage, she realized. By now her face must bear the marks of the emotional wringer that she had been through in the past hour.

"I am prepared to agree that this is a case for provisional liberty," said the judge. "But I would prefer it if someone would undertake to be responsible for Signora Catesby's future appearances at court. However, how is this to be managed in view of her friendless condition?"

"I have found a guarantor that I believe will be acceptable to the court," said Valerio.

Adele stood up and advanced toward the front.

"Is this your guarantor?" said the judge, who evidently recognized her.

"If the court agrees," said Valerio, "I ask that the prisoner be released into the joint custody of Signora Lucci and myself. The Signora will supervise her day-to-day existence, but I shall be responsible for my client's actions and her future appearances at court."

The judge frowned. "What you propose is a very unorthodox arrangement, Advocate Lucci."

"I appreciate that, your honor, and I should like to explain what I have in mind. I own a villa near the outskirts of Florence, which is occupied by the female members of my family, but not by myself. I seldom visit it. My suggestion is that Signora Catesby reside there, in the company of Signora Lucci, until such time as the court requires her further appearance."

"You do not reside in this villa yourself?" the judge repeated.

"I have not done so for fifteen years," said Valerio. "I own it only because it once belonged to my father. It is now occupied by my grandmother, my mother and my sister." He said the last words with slow emphasis, ensuring that the entirely female character of the villa was not lost on anybody.

The judge turned his attention to Adele. "Are you willing to assume this responsibility, *signora*?" Adele confirmed her willingness in brief formal words. The judge drummed his fingers on the desk, lost in thought. Helena could feel her heart beating painfully. At last the judge turned to her.

"Are you agreeable to this arrangement, Signora Catesby?"

"I am agreeable," she heard herself say.

"Very well. I will permit this since it appears to be the only alternative to custody." He fixed hard eyes on Valerio. "I permit it, Advocate Lucci, only because your own reputation as a man of honor is such as to command the court's respect. I also impose a condition that the prisoner must report to the police every day. The police will retain her passport." His voice dropped and Helena thought she heard him mutter, "Although that appears to have very little effect."

There was a scraping of chairs and a loud buzz of conversation rose from the well of the court. Valerio took Helena firmly by the arm and shepherded her from the court. She went with him, still hardly able to believe the incredible events of the last two minutes. Adele had disappeared.

Valerio stayed with her while the formalities of her release were completed. She answered questions and signed papers like an automaton. Only the surface of her mind was aware of what she was doing. The rest was reeling under the impact of the morning's events. Brian, whom she had believed so kind and loyal, had abandoned her to save his own skin. Valerio was calmly taking her into his own home as though it was the most natural thing in the world. The whole world felt as if it had been turned upside down.

At last Valerio took her by the arm and led her to the front entrance, where a sleek black car was waiting, with a man at the wheel. It wasn't until she saw Adele sitting in the back that Helena realized where she was being taken. So far she hadn't been alone with Valerio since the end of the hearing.

"Are you coming too?" she asked him.

"No, I have other clients who need me."

"But I have to talk to you. We can't just leave matters here."

"I shall dine at the villa tonight. We can discuss your case then, *signora*. For now, I want you to get into the car and go home with my grandmother."

He opened the car and stood waiting while she climbed in. Then the door slammed shut and the car was moving. She turned her head and found Adele looking at her appraisingly. They were shut off from the driver by a glass partition, and she ventured to say, "You do realize who I am, don't you?"

"Of course." Adele nodded. "When Valerio explained what he wanted me to do, he told me everything."

"And you don't mind?"

"Valerio always has good reasons for whatever he does," said the old woman. "Sometimes you only see later what they are."

"Do you know what they are?"

Adele grinned suddenly. "Wait and see. Why do you want reasons, anyway? Isn't it enough that you're free?"

"Yes. I didn't mean to sound ungrateful. I can hardly believe what Valerio has done for me. But how will you feel, having me living under your roof, maybe for a long time?"

"It's Valerio's roof," said Adele. "It's up to him who lives under it."

"Don't tell me that you're a browbeaten little old lady, docilely submitting to the commands of your tyrannical grandson," Helena said with spirit. "I wouldn't believe it! Valerio once told me that you'd live forever, because even St. Peter was afraid of you."

Adele gave a crack of laughter, evidently much pleased by this assessment. "Then I'll tell you something," she said. "It was Valerio's idea that we should both be responsible for you, but that you should actually live with me—that was my suggestion. And I must warn you that it did not find favor with my daughter-in-law. She is not pleased that you enter our house, and I fear that you won't receive a welcome from her."

"Well, I can't blame her for that. She must hate me. Surely you must too?"

Then Adele said something unexpected. "Don't take all the blame, Helena. Women accept blame too easily, and of course men graciously allow us to do so. But if that boy hadn't been a fool, the two of you would have been married long ago."

It was strange to hear the mature, formidable man who had rescued her that morning referred to as "that boy." Stranger still to detect the good-natured contempt in Adele's voice. To her, Valerio was not Advocate Lucci, a brilliant lawyer whose golden tongue could change the fate of others. He was a clown who'd lost the woman he loved by his own clumsiness.

Helena studied her fingers. "Did he ever...marry anyone else?" she asked.

"No," said Adele. "Since then he has never introduced another girl to his family. There have been women, of course; too many, I think. But they have been what my generation would have called 'little friends.' He never mentions marriage."

The car had been climbing while they talked, and now Helena realized that they were within sight of the Villa Lucci. She stared through the window at it, glad to have this chance of hiding the jolt of irrational pleasure that Adele's words gave her.

The villa loomed high over them at the top of the steep hill. The sun was at its height, and a dozen windows of the villa reflected its glare, so that Helena had to shield her eyes. Obviously someone was on the watch for their arrival, for the great iron gates swung open as they approached, and in another minute the car had drawn up outside the front door.

Giorgio, the driver, opened the doors for them, then went to collect Helena's suitcase from the boot. The front door was opened by a large gray-haired woman whom Adele introduced as Nina, the housekeeper. Helena couldn't remember having seen her ten years ago, for which she was grateful.

There was no sign of Maria Lucci, Valerio's mother, and Nina explained, blank-faced, that the *signora* was unwell and would spend the day in her room. Adele snorted and commanded Helena to accompany her. Followed by Giorgio with the suitcase they went up to the second floor, and Adele led the way into a large bedroom. It was dark as they entered, possibly because the shutters were drawn to protect the room from the noon glare. But even when Adele had thrown the shutters open, half the room was still poorly lit.

The chief item of furniture was a large, four-poster bed, hung with old, faded tapestries. Plainly this was the best guest room and Helena realized that somebody—presumably Adele—had gone to a lot of trouble to ensure that she was well treated. Although she found the dimness oppressive, Helena thanked her with real warmth. She was all too aware that she might have been spending tonight in a cell.

"I will have some lunch sent up to you," said Adele, "and then you rest this afternoon. We dine early, and you must look good."

She insisted on going through Helena's suitcase to see what she had that was suitable. She seized on her one evening dress, a pale green chiffon, simply cut and very elegant. Helena stiffened. "I can't wear that," she said at once. "Surely it's too formal?"

"No. When Valerio comes here we dress for dinner."

"But it's the dress I was wearing when..."

"Hmm!" Adele studied the material. "No matter," she announced at last. "It's crumpled, but not damaged. I will give it to the maid. You'll have it back in time."

She seemed satisfied that this answered all problems, and Helena didn't know how to tell her that she was loath to wear that dress again. She discovered that Valerio had been right about his grandmother. Her decisiveness had the power of a whirlwind.

When she was alone Helena wandered around the room. She packed away her clothes in the vast walnut wardrobe and chest of drawers. One door, she found, led to her own bathroom, a large echoing chamber, lined with old-fashioned tiles. While she was studying it the maid came in with her lunch on a tray. As soon as she was alone again Helena flung back the curtains to get some light into the room, and froze at what she saw.

There were bars on the window.

For a long moment she stood staring at them, white-faced. Then the truth dawned on her, and she collapsed onto the window seat, laughing shakily at herself. The bars were old and rusty, and shaped in decorative scrolls. They had obviously been there for years as a protection against burglars. There were similar bars on the windows of every big house in Florence.

She pulled herself together and settled down to eat, telling herself not to give way to fancies. But her thoughts whirled in confusion. She'd woken this morning, convinced that by nightfall she would be locked in a cell. Instead she found herself a guest in the house where once she had nearly been the mistress, a prisoner of Valerio Lucci.

She tried to push the thought away. Of course she wasn't a prisoner. But shut away in Valerio's house she knew she was totally vulnerable to him. He'd said he was not vengeful, but she knew him to be a proud man. And she'd struck a savage blow at that pride in front of half Florence. No matter that it was ten years ago. The Italian *vendetta* never sleeps.

Could any man be as generous and forbearing as he had seemed today? Might it not be a mask for something more sinister? He wouldn't punish her by losing her case; an action like that would harm his own reputation. But in this house he had her at his mercy, possibly for as long as a year. He might do what he liked and toss her back into police custody if she protested. If she complained to the world, he would call her a liar. And whom would the world believe? Now that Brian had defected she was alone and friendless and totally in Valerio's power.

Suddenly, perversely, she felt strength flowing back into her. With her back to the wall there was nothing to do but turn and fight, and the knowledge heightened her courage. She was glad now that Adele had insisted on her wearing the evening dress. For the past few days Valerio had seen her as a victim, but that was over. If she had to fight him, she'd do it in full war paint and with all her weapons at the ready. The first step would be a long, refreshing soak. As she headed for the bathroom she snatched off the bandage.

Six

In the early evening Nina came to fetch Helena downstairs for dinner. She entered the big salon where she'd had dinner ten years ago, to find Adele standing in the window with a young woman that she did not immediately recognize. It was the girl who turned first, advancing on Helena with hand outstretched. "Hello," she said gruffly. "You won't remember me. I'm Serena."

"Of course. You were a little girl, ten years old."

Serena had grown into a big, strapping woman, handsome rather than pretty, and with an air of confidence that made her seem older than she was. The little girl who'd once questioned Helena with childish eagerness now towered over her by three inches. Helena found herself asking the questions, and discovered that Serena was at university, studying law. In the holidays she did shorthand and typing in her brother's office, "picking up whatever I can."

"That's unusual in Italy, isn't it?" said Helena. "A woman lawyer?"

"There's more of us than there used to be, but still not too many," Serena agreed. "Mama nearly fainted when she heard what I wanted to do, but I told her it was the best way to capture a bright young lawyer as a husband. After that she thought it was a good idea."

Helena joined in her laughter, remembering her own brush with Maria Lucci on this subject. She had a feeling that Serena wasn't husband hunting, any more than she had been.

"Mama isn't joining us for dinner," Serena went on. "She's a little tired..."

"I've explained all about that," said Adele, coming forward. She was magnificently dressed in a gown of silver and black. Although she was nearly eighty, it was plain she took as much pleasure in dressing extravagantly as she had in her youth. Serena was dressed in a severely tailored dark dress, with her black hair pulled back so that the magnificent sculptured lines of her head were evident. Next to her grandmother she was put somewhat in the shade.

Beside them Helena was glad she had worn the green chiffon dress. She'd managed to hide the bruise on her cheek, and arrange her hair so that her forehead was partly covered. It had taken her a full hour to make up her face to her satisfaction, and she'd felt like an ancient Briton applying blue woad in the hope of terrifying the enemy. Now she knew she looked glamorous, and as close as she would ever be to being beautiful. She remembered how Valerio's reading glasses had seemed to cover his face with a protective visor, and realized that she'd done the same.

After a few minutes Valerio arrived, handsome and elegant in white embroidered evening shirt and dark suit. She was immediately aware of his shock when he saw her, although only someone who knew him well could have read the barely perceptible hesitation in his manner. It was strange to have that intimate knowledge of a man who was essentially a stranger.

She knew that she too must be a stranger to him. Her figure had filled out, and the slight angularity of her teen years was gone. So was her youthful "unformed" look, and the childlike, eager joy that he had loved so much. Of the girl she had once been, only the courage and passionate intensity remained. Now she looked what she was—a woman who had learned to survive the pain of her life, who had faced the death of youthful hopes, but clung on to her integrity; a woman who valued the experience of her senses, but did not depend on it; who intrigued men but had learned to distrust their pursuit, and keep herself at a wary distance from them.

Valerio frowned when he saw that his mother was not present. He excused himself politely to Helena, and vanished upstairs. After a few minutes he returned.

"My mother hopes you will forgive her absence, *signora*," he said to Helena. "But her poor health prevents her from greeting you."

"Of course," she said hastily, and was glad that Nina's announcement of dinner prevented her from having to say more.

Over dinner the talk turned to the events of the morning, and Helena became aware of an unusual mood in Valerio. He was exhilarated by his victory, alive with a brilliant inner light that illuminated but did not warm him.

"The real stroke of luck was Ferone," he said. "Having the prosecution appoint that buffoon was the kind of gift that normally only comes with Christmas. He did everything perfectly, relied on an unreliable witness, neglected to prepare his case properly and antagonized the judge. I could hardly have asked for more."

Helena cast her mind back to her previous knowledge of Valerio. In the past when his happiness and pleasure had overflowed it had been because he was with her. Then, too, she had seen this light that came from deep within him. But it had glowed, not dazzled as it did now, and it had been full of warmth, because it flowed from his love.

Was this what had happened to him, what she had done? Had the chill that had once been only on the surface now enveloped his very heart, so that he could find pleasure only in his ambitions?

When the meal came to a close Valerio drank only one cup of coffee before pushing his chair back and saying, "I'm afraid I must leave you early tonight. *Signora*, there are a few matters concerning your case that I would like to discuss with you before I depart. You will excuse us, Adele?"

In the hallway he stopped and looked at her bare shoulders.

"I was going to suggest that we go outside, but perhaps you won't be warm enough?"

"It's a lovely evening, I'll be fine," she assured him.

The grounds of the Villa Lucci were enchanted. Whoever had landscaped them had turned the steep slope into an advantage. The path that led downward wound in long loops like a mountain road. At every turn trees shielded the vista till the last moment, then parted to reveal new curiosities. Small side paths appeared and disappeared without warning.

Valerio took her down one of these to where it broadened out into a circular patch of ground. In the center of this was a low, round table with one central leg. It seemed to have been sculpted from one large piece of stone. Near it were three long benches also made from stone, curved to follow the line of the table. On the house side this little arbor was completely shielded by trees. On the far side there was a view of Florence, where the first lights of evening were becoming visible.

"I'm glad to see you looking so much recovered from your ordeal," Valerio said when she had seated herself. "I'm sorry it was necessary for me to go about it by such a method, but there was no other way, as I hope you appreciate."

"I did in the end," she admitted. "I didn't like it when you suggested that I was hiding something, though, and I still don't like it. I don't see what it gained."

"It made the judge believe in your amnesia," said Valerio. "That was your vulnerable point, and Ferone was bound to attack it. But when I—and then the judge—offered you the chance to save yourself by 'remembering' something against Brian Hanley, and you refused to take it, the judge was impressed. You either had to be an incredibly naive innocent, unjustly taking the blame, or you had to have genuinely lost your memory of those few hours. Either way it worked in your favor.

"You did exactly the right thing. By refusing to save yourself at his expense you underlined the extent of his betrayal of you. Italy is an old-fashioned country. It expects a certain level of chivalry toward a woman. A man who runs for it and leaves the woman to face trouble alone is an object of disgust.''

He was sitting opposite her, one foot resting on the low table, an arm resting on his knee. He was looking away from her as he spoke these last words, his eyes fixed on the view across the city, where the lights were appearing faster now as the light faded. They were in semidarkness now, and she could hardly make out his face.

''Do you really think Brian is guilty?'' she said.

''You must be totally besotted with him if you can ask such a question,'' he said coldly. ''Can there be any doubt after his behavior? He made very sure of getting to you before the police did. Your amnesia must have seemed like a windfall to him—it allowed him to plant his version in your head. Did you suspect nothing then?''

''How could I? I just thought how kind he was being, especially when he wanted to stay with me when the policeman came in.''

''Of course. He wanted to hear what you had to say, and head you off from any dangerous recollections. Really, Helena, where were your wits?''

''That's not fair!'' she said hotly. ''I'd just come round after being unconscious for hours, and I had no reason to suspect him.''

''Of course,'' he said, after a short silence. ''I beg your pardon. But this man's true character is so obvious to me that it pains me to see you so deluded.''

''Well, I'm not deluded anymore,'' she said in a bitter voice. ''Whatever the truth about that night, the fact that he ran away and then issued that dreadful statement trying to make me sound like some stupid female who'd been throwing herself at him—after the number of times he's said he loved me—'' She became silent with anger.

''It is never wise to believe protestations of love,'' said Valerio lightly. ''However convincing they sound at the time, events frequently prove them to have been hollow.''

Through the deceptively casual tone, Helena could detect an undertone of bitterness that shook her. After so many years,

Valerio's feelings were still those that had made him shut his door against her frantic hammering. But something in Helena backed away from a confrontation at this moment, and when she broke the long silence, it was to take up only the superficial meaning of his words.

"They never did sound very convincing. He just thought if he talked about it enough he could talk me into his bed. He never managed it, and I was never fooled, but I did think he was kind and decent."

"Yes, you told me," said Valerio. He showed no sign of reaction to her declaration that she'd never slept with Brian; she wondered just what kind of reaction she'd expected. Why did it even matter that he should know? But obscurely she felt that it was important.

"Did you really not know of his previous convictions?" he went on. "You were very convincing, but it struck me as unlikely. He's only been an M.P. for a year, hasn't he? Didn't the papers rake it up then?"

"No, but that's not so surprising. There's a law in England that protects people from that and since no one was actually hurt, his convictions would count as 'minor' offenses. After all this time they'd be legally wiped out. How did you find out about them?"

"You gave me the clue when you told me how he'd hurried to see you before the police. It might have been the innocent loyalty you evidently believed it, or it might be more sinister. The more I found out about what he'd planted in your mind, the more suspicious I got.

"After that it was a question of consulting British records to discover details. Luckily there is a brotherhood among lawyers, so I had help. When I knew the dates it was easy to look up the back issues at the local newspaper offices. I was served by an elderly clerk who gave me the stats I asked for without a murmur. I don't think he'd ever heard of the law you describe. And of course it is not the law in Italy, so there was nothing to stop my introducing the evidence here."

"I haven't thanked you yet. You did a marvelous detective job."

He shrugged. "Your real thanks should be directed to Brian Hanley himself. If he hadn't run away you'd have been in a much weaker position. As it is, there's enough suspicion on him to keep you free until your own memory returns."

"Or until Lucilla Dorani wakes up and clears me."

"Don't hope for that. She's in a deep coma. It might last for a long time, perhaps for months. And who knows what she'll be able to remember when she wakes? You are your own best hope. You *must* try to remember something!"

"And suppose I remember enough to show that I'm really guilty after all?"

"I don't believe it. If you are guilty, why did Brian Hanley invite suspicion by escaping?"

"Perhaps he just didn't want to be a witness against me?" Helena said stubbornly. "He did say in that statement that he didn't think I was drunk when I took the wheel."

Valerio made a sound of impatience. "Will nothing make you admit the truth about this man? Of course he said that you seemed to be sober, otherwise he would have been blamed for letting you drive. Have you forgotten what lengths he went to to convince *you* that you'd been drinking? But there are none so blind as those who will not see. In some senses it is lucky that you are so foolishly in love with him. It helped to persuade the judge that it was safe for you to live here."

"I'm not in love with Brian," she said firmly.

"And yet you've considered marrying him, haven't you?"

"Yes, well..."

In the semidarkness Valerio laughed softly. "You're right. The two don't always go together."

"I thought it would be one of those safe marriages," she said. "Marriage to a nice kindly man that I could rely on. That sounds rather funny now."

"The only true safety is to be found in love," he said unexpectedly, "and not always even there. What about your husband? Were you in love with him?"

"I thought I was when I married him, but I think I partly talked myself into it. I was lonely, and I wanted someone to love...." Her voice faltered for a moment. "He was an artist

too, so I persuaded myself we'd understand each other." She
gave a mirthless laugh. "It didn't last long. We were only together for three years; at that point I couldn't bear his endless
infidelities. I used to wonder why he married me. He said he'd
thought for a while that I was the one who could make him
settle down. By the time he'd found out I wasn't, it was too late.
Those were his very words." Helena's mouth twisted in bitterness. "He said that once we were married I'd turned into just
another woman, no more interesting than the rest."

*In my eyes you are already my wife and above all other
women.* The words seemed to be there between them, as though
the ghost of the young Valerio had spoken from the past,
commenting ironically on the man she had chosen above
himself.

"He used to say that he needed the excitement of love affairs," she went on, "and as a fellow artist I ought to understand that."

"Thus freeing you to have affairs of your own," Valerio
commented dryly, "without guilt."

"I didn't see it that way," she declared. "He said much the
same thing, and I think it would have suited him if I'd had affairs, but I'm not made like that. It would have been a kind of
death to me."

"And yet you too feel that an artist needs the excitement of
the senses, don't you, Helena?" he said ironically. "My mistake was in not understanding earlier my true role in your life—
not a husband, but an enlargement of your experience."

"That isn't true, Valerio. I loved you. But I was too young
to know what I wanted. If only we'd met when I was older,
everything might have been different." She hoped desperately
that he'd understand.

"Or if I'd been prepared to wait on your pleasure for a few
years," he said bitingly.

"Why didn't you open the door to me that day? I could have
explained, made you forgive me—"

He turned on her suddenly, and in the dim light she could see
his eyes burning like hot coals. *"Forgive you?* Will you ever
understand what you did? Half of Florence knew we had been

lovers. When you walked out on me in the face of them all, do you know what they said of me? I won't tell you the word. It's too indecent for a woman's ears. But the gist of it was that you'd passed judgment on me in bed, and the judgment hadn't been favorable. Can you appreciate what that means in this country?

"Once, soon afterward, a man I knew made the sign of horns to me in the street. I dealt with him, and no man ever dared repeat his mistake. But you did that to me, *you*, to whom I had offered my heart, my life and everything I was. *Forgive you?*"

"Valerio, I didn't realize—I'm..."

"Do not," he said harshly, "say to me that you are sorry. Those ridiculous words would be more than I could endure."

"But I didn't want to walk out on you in front of everyone," she pleaded. "I called you that morning; I tried to warn you. I begged you not to go to the church, Valerio, but you wouldn't listen to me. I tried everything but I couldn't make you realize that I was serious."

"No, I couldn't believe that you would do such a thing to me," he said somberly. "I thought that you loved me."

"But don't you see, if you'd believed me that morning, we could have talked to everyone *together*, and said it was a joint decision to call the wedding off. You wouldn't have had that wait in the church. And if we'd gone on living together afterward, everyone would have seen that I hadn't 'passed judgment on you.'"

"And do you think that I would have wanted to go on living with you afterward, Helena? Even after your nice, neat little 'joint announcement,' which you seem to imagine would have solved everything. For me our love was sacred. It meant marriage and children, and a life together. Once I finally understood that it didn't mean these things to you, what reason would I have had to stay with you? Do you think I have so little pride that I would have lived with you 'on probation,' hoping that one day my turn might come?"

"No, it wouldn't have worked, would it?" she said wretchedly. "It was my fault for letting it all get so far. But it was your fault too, for rushing me. I tried to tell you, many times, that I wasn't ready. But you just rode roughshod over me."

"I didn't think that offering my life to you came under the heading of 'riding roughshod,'" he replied coldly. "It is pointless to discuss this further, *signora*. We shall never agree on this matter. I am to blame for having raised the subject. It will not occur again."

"But now we've started to talk, can't we finish?" she said. "There's so much I—"

"The subject is closed," he said, with a gesture that was meant to silence her.

"It most certainly is not!" she snapped, infuriated by this dictatorial attitude. "You've had your say, but the minute I try to show you my point of view 'the subject is closed.' You're very good at not listening to what doesn't suit you. If you'd listened to me on the morning of your wedding—"

"Of our what?" he queried ironically.

"Or if you'd listened to me earlier, when I tried to tell you I wasn't ready, it need never have happened. I'm sorry you were hurt, Valerio, but I'm damned if I'm going to be cast in the role of villain. I was seventeen. You were older, and far more mature. You were the one who should have known better.

"I did you a favor that day. If I'd gone ahead with the wedding we'd be divorced by now—"

"Never," he broke in, "for I would never have let you go. Divorce isn't as easy in this country as in yours. You couldn't have divorced me without serious grounds, which you wouldn't have had. And I would not have divorced you, ever."

"Don't you realize that you're making our marriage sound like a prison?" she said passionately. "That's why I ran away from you. In the end I would still have run away. If I couldn't divorce you I'd have left you, because I had to find out the answers for myself."

"Well, you left me. Did you find the answers?"

"Yes, I did. You were right. I'm not a great artist; I'm a very competent one. But I can live with that because I found it out for myself. What I couldn't have endured was not knowing."

He shrugged. "You have no regrets then?"

She wondered what he would say if she told him of the regrets, of how she had measured all other men against him and found them wanting. Even when she'd first been infatuated with Gary she'd known, in her heart of hearts, that he was second best. Would Valerio laugh now if he knew how she'd discovered, too late, that he was her one true love, and cursed the fate that had made them meet too soon?

But she knew there was no way she could tell him this. In their present circumstances it would sound like a cynical offer, the prisoner trying to buy favors from the jailer. If she had nothing else she would keep her self-respect.

"No," she said bleakly. "I have no regrets."

"In that case," he said, rising to his feet, "I can only be glad for you, and there is nothing more to say. Now I must be going."

It was barely nine o'clock, and she wondered why he had to hurry off. It occurred to her that he might be going to spend time with one of the "little friends" that Adele had spoken of, but she pushed the thought away. She'd forfeited the right even to wonder about that. Besides, it hurt too much.

At the door of the villa, he stopped.

"I won't come in again. I'll just say this. You will have to report to the police every day. Giorgio will take you into Florence and bring you back. If you wish to do some shopping he'll accompany you. You must never go into town alone."

"Is that necessary? I may be in your custody, but do I have to spend every moment under your supervision? I'm not going to run away."

"It's necessary for your protection. I don't want to risk your being alone if you encounter Guido Ranelli. You saw how he behaved in the courtroom. Make no mistake. He hates you!

"As for your running away, you could do that without difficulty. The gates of this villa aren't locked during the day. You could get back to England as easily as Brian Hanley did.

"But, you may recall, I have staked my honor and reputation with the court on the promise that you will not run away.

If you fail to make an appearance at the promised time, I am a ruined man. There is an irony in that, is there not, which I am sure you will appreciate. Goodnight, *signora*."

Seven

For the next few days Helena had little time to consider Valerio and his puzzling behavior. She was taken up with finding her feet in the new life that was clearly going to be hers for some time.

At first she saw nothing of Maria. Once, passing near her door while an explosive argument was plainly going on, Helena thought she heard Valerio's mother snap "Not while that woman is in the house!" She hurried away, feeling guilty and uncomfortable. That evening Maria made her first appearance at the dinner table. She greeted Helena with frigid courtesy, regretted that her poor health had made it impossible for her to meet her earlier and ignored her thereafter. Here was a hostility, Helena realized, that wasn't going to be easily overcome, if ever.

Adele's attitude was the reverse of her daughter-in-law's. She took trouble to be friendly toward Helena, and make her feel at home. Whether she was doing this only for Valerio's sake, or for her own reasons, she evidently bore no ill-will.

Serena seemed to be halfway between them. Her manner was pleasant, but there was a gruff wariness about it that told Helena she was reserving judgment.

Every day Giorgio took Helena into Florence to report to the police, and saw her back home. Each time Helena looked around for any sign of Guido Ranelli. She never saw him, which surprised her after his outburst in the courtroom, and Valerio's warning. But when the police sergeant grew more used to her he told her that Lucilla Dorani was still in a coma, and Guido spent much of his time at her bedside. Helena began to fear that Valerio's prediction might be correct, and the girl would never recover. Her own memory remained obstinately silent, suspending her in limbo for a time that seemed to stretch eternally ahead.

Her stock of money was running low, but she used some of the remainder to buy a large sketchbook and some charcoal. After that she spent every afternoon in the grounds of the villa, for there was plenty there to delight her.

The villa itself was an extraordinary building. It reminded her of an elaborately iced cake with its masses of decorative stonework, its balustrades, its Gothic windows and its battlements. It was built in three stories, but at one corner it rose still further into an octagonal tower.

Helena sketched the villa from every possible angle. It was a challenging subject because the steepness of the land meant that every view was from below. When she felt she'd exhausted her inventiveness on the house she turned to the grounds, which were equally intriguing. Here too there were stone balustrades, leading to broad stone steps guarded at the bottom by stone lions.

At the bottom of the slope the ground broadened out to encompass a very small lake, at the side of which was built a tiny temple, decorated with figures. When she examined these more closely Helena was amazed to discover that they were Egyptian. The entrance to the temple was guarded by six tiny sphinxes. None of them looked very old, and she concluded that some previous owner of the villa had been an eccentric.

Adele confirmed this. "They were put there by my husband's great-grandfather. He bought them from an Englishman who had lived in Egypt. The Englishman had them made for his home in England, and then changed his mind. So now they are here."

"I like that," said Helena, laughing. "This whole house intrigues me." She was feeling less oppressed by the gloom now, as though by capturing the house on paper she had somehow brought it under her control.

"My husband's family has lived here for five hundred years," said Adele. "Of course, when it was first built, it didn't look like this. But the core of that first house is still here, and the rest had been built around it. So many things have happened here, so many people have been born and loved each other and died."

"I wish I knew more about them," said Helena. It crossed her mind that if she understood Valerio's family she might find the clue to him.

"That is very simple," said Adele. "There's a family history in the library. It has been written over the centuries by the women of the family, and every generation has added to it."

Later that day Helena went on a solitary exploration of the house, including the third story, which was mostly empty. But when she came to the door that led into the octagonal tower she found it locked. Every other door had opened to her touch, but this one couldn't be budged. Probably, she thought, the stairs into the tower were unsafe, and this was a precaution.

It was late afternoon by then, so she went back to her room and found that while she had been gone someone had delivered the family history. The five volumes were standing on the table by her bed. She opened one casually and soon became so absorbed that she was almost late for dinner.

The days began to run together. The first week was over, then the second. When she ran out of subjects to sketch in the grounds and house, she turned her attention to its occupants. She did the three women from memory and was surprised to discover a family resemblance that united them to Valerio, something she hadn't noticed before. It occasionally hap-

pened that way, she knew. One's fingers reproduced something that one's mind had recorded only subconsciously.

She was now on friendly terms with Giorgio, and every
morning after she had reported to the police, the two of them
would adjourn to a nearby wine bar. Here Giorgio was a general favorite, and one morning, sensing that he would prefer to
linger among his cronies, she said impulsively, "Look, I want
to browse around the shops for a while. Why don't you stay
here? I'll meet you here in an hour."

He was willing enough, but made her promise not to be later
than an hour. Helena hurried away, feeling truly free for the
first time since she'd woken up in the hospital. She looked
round some shops, bought herself a cup of coffee and arrived
back at the wine bar with two minutes to spare. After that it
became an understood thing between them that they would
separate and meet again for the return journey. Gradually one
hour became two. Helena never saw Guido Ranelli, and she
concluded that Valerio was being overcautious. That was the
sop she offered her conscience for deceiving him.

Twice a week Valerio came to dinner. Those were the hard-
est times of all for Helena, for the sight of him sitting opposite
her at table, an impersonal stranger, was increasingly painful.
At the end of the evening he would always have a brief private
talk with her, but he never again lowered his guard and talked
of their past as he'd done that first evening.

Sometimes she wondered why he talked to her privately at all.
He said nothing that could not have been said before the others, or over the telephone. It occurred to her that he was trying
to confirm their new distant relationship, both in her mind and
his own. If so, she had to accept it. They were strangers now,
by her actions and by his wish.

Yet it was hard to think of him as a stranger when she knew
details about him that only a lover could know. She knew the
silly things, such as that he had one foot half a size larger than
the other and never wore nylon because it irritated his skin. She
knew he always drank red wine, never white, because white
gave him a headache. She knew that his one secret vanity was

his shapely hands, which he always kept scrupulously manicured.

She knew him intimately too. He was a stranger, but she knew that the little hollow at the base of his throat was extrasensitive, and the soft touch of her lips there could drive him wild. He was the professional man to his fingertips, correct and austere, but there was nothing correct or austere about his lovemaking. In bed his propriety fell away from him like an unwanted garment, and he could claim a woman's body with all the uninhibited abandon that was repressed in his daily life.

They were strangers, yet she knew his smooth chest and flat stomach, with the scar of a childhood operation, and just below it the dark, curly hair in which nestled her delight. Even now that he was slightly heavier she knew him well enough to imagine the look and feel of his narrow hips and his firm, neat behind.

But more than the look of his body, she knew its reactions. She knew where he loved to be kissed, and which caresses teased him most. She knew how he could be aroused by a word or a look, and how that arousal could be unmistakably imprinted on his features, visible to a woman who could read the signs. She knew everything about him—except what he was truly thinking and feeling. Because they were strangers.

One morning as she got into the car, Giorgio said, "Signor Lucci says I am to take you to his office this morning. He has some letters for you."

She was intrigued. She had never visited Valerio in his office before, although she knew where it was. She had passed it every time she had gone to his apartment, and had often wondered what lay behind that discreet, shabby door.

They went first to the police, and then Helena directed Giorgio to call at the nearest bank, for her money was almost at an end. She handed her international credit card to the cashier and said she wanted to draw the lire equivalent of 150 pounds. The cashier typed something on a computer keyboard, then stared at the screen, frowning. "I'm sorry, *signora*," he said at last. "There are instructions against paying out any money to you."

"But that's impossible," she said, bewildered. "I'm not nearly up to my credit limit yet. I've still got about five hundred pounds available to me."

The cashier typed again. "The result is the same, *signora*," he said. "A stop has been put on your account. There is no mistake."

She sat tight-lipped in the car on the way to Valerio's office. Whatever happened she wouldn't let him see how upset she was. But this new blow had left her with just ten pounds in her purse. Now she was more than ever dependent on Valerio's charity, and the thought galled her.

As soon as she was inside the downstairs hall of Valerio's office she had to stop and blink. After a moment she grew used to the dim light, and realized that Giorgio was pointing toward a flight of stairs. As she approached it she became aware of a heavy line in the wall, about ten feet from the floor.

"This is the watermark," said Giorgio when he saw her looking at it. "When the floods came, that is the level the water reached. All over Florence you can see those marks. People preserve them to remind them what they suffered, and to warn them never to let the river burst its banks again."

This was the thing that had changed Valerio's life, she thought, running her fingertips over the line. But for those floods he would never have become a lawyer. He'd have been an art dealer, as he wanted to be, and they'd have met in other circumstances, and everything might have been different.

She snatched her hand away and firmly told herself to stop. There was no point in letting her thoughts drift on in this fashion. What was done was done. She had chosen her path, away from Valerio, and she would not—*could not*—allow herself the weakness of regrets.

The people they had once been were dead. The people they might have become together would never exist. The man and woman who lived in their place were strangers, forced by circumstances to be allies, but no more. They could carry their joint burden of painful memories only by averting their eyes from it.

Valerio's office turned out to be very much larger inside than the exterior had suggested. It also housed two other advocates, both of whom, Helena later learned, were distant cousins. But without doubt it was Valerio who dominated.

Serena was sitting at a typewriter in a small anteroom. She smiled at Helena and flipped a switch on the intercom on her desk to inform Valerio of Helena's arrival. When his voice on the other end said "Send her in now, please," Serena rose and opened a nearby door.

Valerio looked up from his papers, and stood at the sight of her. He was wearing his reading glasses, which contributed to his air of severity, but his manner was cordial enough as he waved her to a seat and offered her a coffee. Helena saw two letters lying on the front of his desk. She seated herself and picked them up, turning them over in her hands. From the addresses printed on the envelopes she could see that one came from her credit-card company, and one from Hanley Leather Goods.

Valerio finished pouring coffee from a percolator and set the cup on the desk in front of her. "They arrived at the British consulate," he said. "I said I'd give them to you. It might be better if you read them here. If it's bad news there may be something we should discuss." His voice betrayed nothing but quiet, impersonal courtesy.

Helena tore open the letter from the credit-card company. It was frostily worded and declared that since she had left the country, with no prospect of an immediate return, her account was canceled and immediate payment of the outstanding sum was demanded.

The other letter was from the personnel department of Hanley Leather Goods. It stated that since there was no immediate prospect of her returning to work, her employment was terminated. In lieu of notice, three months' pay had been deposited with her bank. The firm was sorry to lose her services as she had always been an efficient and conscientious employee, however, etc. etc. The letter was typewritten and signed by the personnel officer.

Helena stared from one letter to the other, prey to feelings of both shock and disgust. She supposed that she shouldn't be surprised, but they were the final strokes that underlined her loneliness.

Valerio took both letters and studied them. "Well, it was to be expected," he said. "Given the kind of man Brian Hanley is, this must be fairly average behavior for him. Try not to let it bother you."

"Not bother..."

"You couldn't have gone back to work for him anyway," Valerio pointed out reasonably.

"After what he's done, how dare he think he can buy me off with three months' pay!" she snapped.

"What are you going to do? Toss it back on principle?"

It was on the tip of her tongue to say that this was exactly what she was going to do, but she checked herself. She couldn't afford that kind of principle, she realized. If she didn't take Brian's money it meant getting deeper into Valerio's debt, and that thought was intolerable.

"No, I can't do that, can I?" she said bleakly.

Valerio looked at her pale face and stormy eyes. He was about to say something when the buzzer on his intercom went.

"Yes!" he said impatiently.

"Signor Ferrando is here," came Serena's voice.

"Very well. Ask him to wait a few minutes." Valerio flicked the switch and turned back to Helena. "Ferrando is early, so I'm afraid you can't stay. Please tell my mother that I'll be joining you all for dinner at the villa this evening. We can talk then."

He ushered her out and into the care of Giorgio. For the journey home she got into the back of the car, instead of sitting companionably next to Giorgio as she normally did. She didn't feel like talking. She was trying to come to terms with the feeling of being cast adrift in a vast, hostile sea. Each time something happened she managed to rise to the occasion, but only for a short while. Then some new development would occur and she would have to start again.

But at least, she thought with a faint feeling of relief, she wasn't struggling alone. In the evening Valerio would be there, and his strong, reliable presence would infuse her with new courage.

Even so there was a heavy weight on her heart as she dressed for dinner that evening. She'd spent the afternoon trying to bludgeon some response from her memory, and the result had been only an agony of frustration.

She donned the chiffon evening dress, as she had for the previous times Valerio had dined at the villa. She wished she could change her appearance but she still had only the clothes she'd originally brought with her for a four-day stay. The dress left her neck and shoulders bare, and for a moment her hand hovered over a silver filigree pendant that she'd last worn on the night of the accident. Then she put it away. It had been given to her by Brian, and she wanted no reminders of him now.

In the end she picked up a white silk scarf and draped it around her shoulders. She wanted to be alone for a while longer and to escape from the house, and an unusually cool breeze had sprung up.

She made for the arbor with the stone table where she'd been with Valerio on the first night. It was pleasant there, protected from the breeze by the surrounding trees and she sat looking down over the roofs of Florence, burnished a deeper red by the setting sun. She didn't move until she heard footsteps on the path behind her, and turned to find Valerio there.

"I'm afraid I'm a little late," he said. "I called at the hospital on my way here. I wanted to see if I could get a word with Lucilla's doctor, but he was busy. I met Guido though. The poor fellow looks as if he's going to be there for a long time."

"He must be very devoted to her," said Helena in a low voice.

"Completely. If he had his way he'd never let her out of his sight."

"Then how did she come to be at that party with someone else?"

He shrugged. "Who can say? Maybe she got tired of never being allowed out of Guido's sight. He's very protective, and that sometimes makes her impatient. Perhaps impatience made her stupid.''

"She's afraid of him," said Helena suddenly.

"What?" Valerio had seated himself near her. Now he sat forward and stared at her intently. "How do you know that?"

"I don't know. I just do. It's there in my mind—her saying 'Guido mustn't find out.' "

"Don't forget Brian Hanley told you that."

"Yes, he did. But this is different. I can *hear* her saying it in the most desperate, terrified voice."

"*What else?*"

Helena closed her eyes and frowned, but already the picture was flickering out in her mind. Then it faded and there was nothing.

"Don't try to force it," said Valerio. "You'll only drive the memories away if you try to force them."

She took some deep breaths, steadied by his calm, impersonal tone. He might have been a doctor soothing a patient, interested but uninvolved. And that, she supposed, was what a lawyer had to be; a kind of doctor, with care for everyone, and a heart for none. The words he had once spoken to her about detachment came back to her with a hollow ring.

"Do you remember what you once said to me about detachment?" she could not resist asking him.

He frowned as if her train of thought wasn't clear to him, and answered coolly, "I said that you lacked it. But I turned out to be wrong, didn't I? If I'd known then how great a detachment you were capable of, I might have seen what was coming. I realized only later the full truth of something you said to me, about living your life the way you wanted, and never mind anyone else. I thought it was just youthful blindness until you proved that you meant it."

"You really do hate me, don't you?" she said after a moment. "I've only just realized how much."

"You're wrong. I don't hate you now. For a long time I did—I hated you until there was no hate left in me. There's nothing now, neither hate or anything else. I can even acknowledge that some of the blame may be mine, as you said that first evening. I was crazy with love for you, so crazy that I rushed you along faster than you were ready to go. If I had allowed you more time things might have been different. Perhaps you wouldn't be in the trouble you are in now. So you see, I too have some old debts to pay.''

''Don't tell me that you're helping me in order to salve a guilty conscience?''

''As I told you before, I'm helping you primarily because I walked into that hospital room and discovered that you were my client. I'd already undertaken your case by that time, and it was too late to back out. The others are peripheral reasons. Fundamentally you are no different to me from any other client.''

''That isn't true!'' she said fiercely. ''It can't be true, and you know it.''

He sighed. ''Very well, it isn't true. But for God's sake let us try to pretend that it is, otherwise life will be intolerable for both of us.''

After a silence he went on, ''It does us no good to go over the past. Let us say, if you wish, that I am trying to exorcise your ghost. Some day soon I shall marry. I want children, and I have waited too long. You might spare a moment's pity for my future wife. You took the best of me, and she will find herself with the husk that is left. But when I have seen you depart from Italy, a free woman, perhaps I too can begin to be free.''

The pain of imagining Valerio married was so savage and so unexpected that Helena jumped up and walked away from him, feeling her heart beating painfully against her ribs. Another woman would have his babies, and eventually she would also have his love, for Valerio would not long remain indifferent to his children's mother.

She stopped at last at the stone balustrade, leaned back against it and looked at him.

''Does this lady know what a poor bargain she's being offered?'' she said as lightly as she could.

Valerio smiled ironically, as though he recognized the hidden question. ''She does not know, because she does not yet exist," he said. "Before I start my search in earnest, I owe it to her to rid myself of you, once and for all."

She averted her face, lest he read in it the surge of joy she felt on hearing that there was no real woman to torment her with jealousy.

"I'm surprised that you didn't marry earlier if you wanted children," she said.

"Yes, I was more faithful to you than you to me, was I not?"

"Was it really fidelity?"

He raised his hand in a gesture of acknowledgment. "Shall we say that after you I wasn't tempted to try again?"

"Except for the 'little friends,'" she said daringly.

He gave his quiet laugh and rose to his feet. "I suppose my grandmother has been talking. Yes, I haven't lived the life of a monk. I tried other beds, never quite certain whether I was seeking you or fleeing from you. Whatever the answer, you were there, for a very long time afterwards." He had come to stand behind her and his voice was almost in her ear, otherwise she might not have heard the next words, so softly did he say them. "Did your husband's face ever change to mine on the pillow?"

"Yes," she whispered. "Many times."

"And Brian Hanley?"

"I told you," she said harshly, "I never slept with him."

"How can I believe that? I remember, you see. I recall how vital the life of the senses is to you. I remember how you could express physical joy on a canvas; how you could paint inanimate objects bathed in a glowing light that flowed from your senses. I remember that you had the gifts of life and laughter, and I dared to draw near and seek to warm myself by them. Don't tell me that no other man has inspired you to passion. It is too necessary to you." Valerio's voice was vibrant, and she could feel the heat of his breath against her bare shoulder, for the scarf had fallen off when she rose.

"You seem to forget that I'm not a painter anymore," she said in a hard voice. "I am—or was—a designer of leather goods. I haven't touched paints in three years. You don't need passion to inscribe gilt initials on handbags."

Now he would jeer at her, because she had left him to follow a dream that had perished in the face of reality. She waited, shivering, though whether from the chilly breeze or from the strain of standing so close to him she couldn't have said. But the words he spoke were the last she had expected to hear.

"You should not have stopped painting. You lost faith in yourself, and that is a crime. I would not have let it happen."

She turned to stare at him, but Valerio had moved away.

"We should be going in to dinner," he said in a voice that meant his barriers were in place again. "They will be wondering about us."

He took up her scarf. For a moment he reached toward her, making a movement as if he would drape it around her shoulders.

Then something seemed to happen to him. He stopped abruptly, as though constrained by an unseen hand. Very deliberately he took a step back, folded the scarf and held it out to her. And suddenly she knew that he was afraid. He wanted to touch her; wanted it so desperately that he did not dare to venture even the lightest contact. The memories of their past passion had inflamed him so that the faintest spark would be enough, this minute, to ignite a conflagration that would consume them both.

Her flesh was burning as though his hands had touched it, yet he was more than a foot away from her. Once before, years ago, just being with him had made her feel that she was being passionately kissed, even while he kept his distance.

The same feeling assailed her again, but this time with a violence that left her shaking. Now Valerio wanted to do more than kiss her. It was in his eyes, in the tense lines of his body, that he wanted to strip her naked and repossess what had once been his, to reclaim what he still considered his own, so forcefully and finally that she would be helpless to deny him the total surrender that alone could heal the wound of ten years.

She too had changed from the child who had longed for kisses. This time she was a woman who knew what she wanted, knew every inch of the male body before her, and how it would feel against hers.

Memories of a thousand lovings assailed her. How skillfully his hands had touched her, knowing the intimate caresses that delighted her most; how he had reveled in her ecstatic response because it made him feel one with the gods. It was from this pinnacle that she had cast him down.

She shook her head slightly, trying to force the memories away, but they were too much a part of her, and she had been struggling against them for too long. Now that he was here with her she had no strength to fight the desire that turned her limbs to water.

Her eyes met his in a hypnotic trance, knowing that he was as tormented as she. His mouth had lost its stern, hard expression. The lips were slightly apart, and the breath coming between them was ragged. Across the little distance that separated them she could sense his trembling and knew that his control was stretched to the limit.

His mind might be set against her, his heart might be no longer hers, but his body wanted her as violently and primitively as if the past ten years had never been. Helena knew that she had only to stretch out a hand and touch his face with her fingertips and his iron control would have no more power to restrain him than a cobweb. He would take her there and then on the grass, lost to everything but his consuming need. And afterward he would hate her.

For a long moment she stood motionless, torn apart by longing. At last her breath escaped in a long sigh. "Yes, we should be going inside," she said in a dead voice.

Her words broke the spell. He closed his eyes and opened them again as if coming out of a dream. For a moment it seemed that he wondered where he was. Then he threw her scarf on the table, turned on his heel and left her.

She dropped onto a seat and buried her face in her hands. She wanted to call him back, but she knew he wouldn't come. Now that the moment was gone she passionately regretted that she hadn't reached out to touch him, let the consequences be what they might. Her body ached with the hunger of ten years.

But more than the ache of her flesh was the ache of her heart. It was Valerio who had brought it to life, so long ago, and Valerio for whom it obstinately hungered, deaf to reason, indifferent to the years in between.

And there were so many reasons that she could give her heart why it must not love Valerio. There was the unforgivable wrong that lay between them, the public insult she had offered his sexual pride, as fierce in him as in any other Italian male. The fact that she could still inflame his senses as she had tonight was for him only one more cause for hostility.

But what hurt her the most was the glimpse he had shown her of his heart—ashes burned out on stone. He would not love her because he could no longer love anyone. And this was her doing.

These were the reasons for caution that she could go over again and again, to warn herself against the madness that threatened to engulf her. They were good reasons, solid, wise—and useless.

When she followed him into the house a short while later, Helena found Valerio with his sister, evidently sharing a joke. To her ears his laughter did not ring quite true, but there was no other evidence of their recent encounter.

He looked up when she entered and greeted her in a friendly manner that gave nothing away. The powerful vibrations that had flowed between them just a few minutes ago were dead—so dead that she began to wonder if she had imagined them. She felt as though he had slammed a door shut in her face.

Over dinner he displayed the same chill geniality that he had showed on the evening of the hearing. His manner was impeccable. He spoke humorously to his sister and kindly to his mother. Toward his grandmother his behavior was a combination of flirtation and deference that obviously delighted the old lady.

But to Helena it was all mechanical, as if he had programmed himself to strike the right note with each of them. With herself he adopted a bland courtesy that she knew would be as impenetrable as armor if she were so foolish as to try to get past it. But she did not try. She was sick at heart.

They took coffee in the drawing room. Valerio was engaged in a friendly argument with Adele, with occasional interjections from his mother. Helena gravitated naturally toward Serena, and found herself telling the girl about her letters of the morning. Serena was sympathetic, but took a robustly practical view.

"Take his rotten money, and tell Valerio that you want to sue for some more," she said spiritedly.

"I couldn't do that," said Helena. "But I am going to take it. Tossing it back would cause me more trouble than it would him."

"Good for you. I'm glad you're not going to be 'noble,' because that's just tiresome. When your money comes through we can go into town together and get you some new clothes. You must be bored with living in the few you've got with you."

Helena agreed emphatically and they talked about clothes for a few minutes until Serena said awkwardly, "Look, don't be offended, but would you like to borrow a few things from me, just till you can get your own?"

"I wouldn't if I were you," said Valerio, who had come close enough to overhear. "The two of you are so different, you could never wear each other's things."

Helena remembered that it was one of the endearingly unexpected aspects of Valerio that he had a good eye for feminine adornment. He'd always known exactly what suited her, and during their engagement had been frank about his preferences. It sprang, of course, from the same source as his love of art—his unerring eye for color, line and composition.

"I didn't exactly mean clothes," Serena began to argue. "I meant things like jewelry. I've got a necklace you could wear with that dress. You need some decoration."

"That's true," said Helena, feeling her bare neck. "I do need something here."

"What about that filigree thing of yours?" said Valerio. "It goes perfectly with what you're wearing."

"Brian gave it to me," she said tersely. "I don't particularly want to wear it again. How did you know about it, anyway? I haven't worn it since I've been here."

"You must have. I know I've seen it," he said with a shrug.

"Well, I must have put it on without thinking. I thought I hadn't worn it since the accident. I swear I'll never wear it again."

"Then you must have some of my things," said Serena. "Come upstairs with me now and we'll have a look."

She hurried impulsively away and Helena followed her. When they came down again half an hour later it was to find Adele and Maria sipping coffee alone.

"Valerio had to go," said Adele. "He said I was to say goodnight to you both for him."

Helena smiled, trying to conceal her disappointment, at the same time reproving herself for the feeling. To Valerio she was just another client. He'd said so, and she had to believe it.

She excused herself soon afterward and went up to her room, worn out with the turbulent emotions of the day. She didn't put the light on at once, but went to the window and threw it open, enjoying the view down the hill and onto the rooftops of Florence, flooded in moonlight.

The cool night air struck her bare shoulders, and it was only then that she realized something was missing. The white silk scarf hadn't been with her since she returned to the house. It must still be lying on the table where Valerio had thrown it down.

She decided to fetch it at once. She was too short of clothes to be careless with the ones she had. She could slip quietly out of the house and find her way down to the spot, guided by the brilliant moonlight.

But once out of the house she found that it wasn't so simple. The moonlight illuminated only part of the grounds; the rest was in darkness from the shade of the trees. Then she realized that if she took the path down to below the arbor and climbed back up by one of the side paths she would be well lit all the way.

Once she'd figured that out it was an easy matter to find her way down. The grounds were a mass of silver, unearthly and beautiful in the silence. Even her footsteps, deadened by the grass, made no sound as she turned the corner and began to climb back up to where she could approach the arbor from below. At last she came to a bend in the path, and a moment later she saw the stone table. And at once she stopped, because from this viewpoint she could see what had not been visible from the house.

A man was sitting there, one foot propped on the table, one arm thrown across his knee. The white scarf hung from long, tense fingers that crushed and crushed it again with ceaseless, agitated movements. His head drooped so low that his forehead almost lay on his arm, and his shoulders were slumped in an attitude of utter despair. As Helena watched petrified, breathless, not daring to move, he drew the scarf up and buried his face in the fragrance of its soft folds.

She crept silently away without disturbing him.

Eight

The following afternoon Helena was sketching in the grounds and just thinking it was time to go in, when she saw Serena's little car scoot through the gates and come to an unsteady halt. Serena climbed out and waved to her.

"I'm loaded down," she said as Helena approached. She made a gesture toward the back seat, which was filled with odds and ends. "It's extraordinary how much rubbish you can accumulate in a few weeks in an office."

"Have you finished there now?" said Helena.

"That's right. I go back to university in a couple of weeks and I want to have a short holiday first, so Valerio threw me out of his office and said good riddance," Serena laughed.

"I can just hear him," said Helena wryly. "How does he feel about you being a lawyer? Not too keen, I should think."

"Now there you're wrong, oddly enough. It was really he who talked Mama round. That surprised me a bit, because there's no doubt my dear brother is rather old-fashioned. But then, you never really know what he's thinking. That reminds me—" she began to rummage in her bag "—he gave me something to give you. He couldn't give it to you himself because he's going away for a fortnight.''

"Away?'' said Helena, dismayed. "Do you know where?''

"Not exactly. He said he felt entitled to a holiday like everyone else, and nothing much will be happening in the courts till the summer is really over. It's a bit unexpected, though. Ah, here we are.'' She pulled out an envelope and handed it to Helena. It was heavy, and through the paper Helena could feel a small metal object.

When she was alone Helena tore open the envelope and tipped the contents into her hand. The small object was a key, and wrapped around it was a note in Valerio's firm hand.

I told you that I would have kept you on your true road as an artist. When you have used this key, you will understand. It opens the door to the tower. Whatever you find there is yours.

There was no heading and no signature.

Helena was up the stairs in a moment. The key jammed in the lock, as though it was a long time since it had been used. Then it turned abruptly and she entered the tower, breathlessly climbing the stairs. At the top was another closed door, but this wasn't locked, and she flung it open. Then she stopped dead.

She was in the largest, sunniest, best-equipped artist's studio she'd ever seen. The room occupied the entire top floor of the tower, and had windows in every one of its eight walls. Even now, at sunset, it was flooded with light. On the side that looked down over Florence the floor rose two steps, making a large dais, on which stood an easel. Canvases of every size stood stacked against the wall.

In the main body of the room were chests of drawers. Helena pulled them open feverishly and discovered in them every possible color medium that an artist could want. There were oil paints, watercolors, tempera, gouache, crayons, colored pencils.

Sketchbooks, lead pencils, charcoal, pen and ink all came to light as Helena went from one chest of drawers to another.

Then she came to the shelves lined with books to delight an artist's heart. There were the lives of great artists, explanatory works on technique, books of instruction. The room was more than a studio. It was an Aladdin's cave, a place of enchantment filled with delights. But its real magic lay in the love with which it had been assembled.

"So now you know."

Helena whirled at the sound of the voice from the doorway, for she hadn't known anyone was there. Maria Lucci had entered the room quietly and had been watching her while she rummaged around. Now Maria came forward.

"He did this for you," she said, with a gesture that indicated the entire studio and its contents. "He was going to give it to you as a surprise when you returned from your honeymoon. He said you needed a refuge where you could still be yourself. I did not understand this. We had accepted you into our family. Why should you need more? But he insisted that this was necessary to you."

So Valerio had understood all the time. Sick at heart, Helena stood silent, feeling as though someone had punched her in the stomach, while Maria looked around the room and continued to talk in a cold voice, full of condemnation. "I remember his joy at the thought of how it would please you, how eager he was to see your eyes when he offered you his gift. I watched his face as he made plans, and I saw on it an expression of total happiness and trust that I have never seen on it since."

"How could I have known?" pleaded Helena. "I thought he didn't take me seriously. He told me once I'd never be a really great artist. He said I might be 'successful' as a portrait painter."

"I doubt that," said Maria cruelly. "I've seen the sketches that you've done since you came into this house. Have you not observed, *signora*, that you are drawing the same face over and over again?"

"Yes, I know they all come out looking like Valerio," said Helena. "I thought there must be a strong family resemblance that I'd only noticed at the back of my mind."

"There is no family resemblance," said Maria contemptuously. "Tell me, *signora*, are you familiar with the works of Emile Zola?"

"Some of them," said Helena, bewildered at this turn in the conversation.

"Perhaps you have read *Thérèse Raquin*? If not you should read it. It is about a man, an artist, who commits murder. And ever afterward, when he tries to paint a portrait, the face on his canvas is that of the man he has killed. You killed my son, *signora*. You killed him inside. What has walked and talked in his shape since then has not been a living man." Her voice rose to a cry. "May God forgive you for what you did to him that day! You broke his heart, and he was never the same again!"

She turned and strode out without giving Helena a chance to reply. Helena went to the window and stood looking down over the city. Of all the things that had happened to her in the past weeks, this was the most devastating, the most confusing. She longed to talk to Valerio and ask him the real meaning of what she had found in the tower, but he had carefully removed himself.

She knew now that what had happened between them the previous evening had been no illusion. Valerio had been so deeply affected that he had fled to escape danger. And he'd sent her the key only when he was safely out of the way, because he didn't want to face her questions.

She smiled slightly in self-mockery as she remembered her thoughts on the first day. She'd wondered then if Valerio would use his position to take some kind of advantage of her, but she'd reckoned without his old-fashioned sense of honor. It was she who longed to reach out to him, and he who wished to avoid her. When she had surprised him in the garden last night she'd known that she mustn't let him suspect that she had witnessed his agony. It hadn't been meant for her eyes, and he wouldn't forgive her for surprising him. She had left him alone in the garden, but the temptation to take him in her arms and let her tenderness enfold him had almost overwhelmed her.

And on top of this had come the shock of today's discovery; a new, incredible thought was struggling to form itself in her mind.

She'd left Valerio because she had to discover the truth about herself as an artist—and the truth she'd discovered was bleak. She'd made no great career. Delving into herself she'd found only mediocrity and she'd declared proudly that she'd live with that because it was a truth she'd discovered for herself.

But suppose it wasn't the only possible truth?

She'd taken dead-end jobs because she'd had to. She'd married a husband who spent her precious little store of money and then put his feet up while she went out to work to support him. The cost of the divorce had fallen largely on her. With a mountain of debts to pay she'd settled for work that was safe, and her real talents had become submerged. If she'd married Valerio, she now knew she could have given them freer rein. In this studio that he had put together for her with such love and care she could have developed her skills, free from distracting worries. What truth would she have discovered then?

She had left him to embark on what had been meant to be a voyage of discovery, and she'd sailed into a dead end. How strange if, after all, it might have been through their marriage that she could have found the wide open sea!

As a very small child Helena had sat in nursery school, listening to the story of St. George and the dragon. It had filled her with disgust. While the other little girls had happily drunk in the tale of the beautiful maiden, so romantically rescued at the last moment, Helena had roundly declared that the maiden was "soppy"; she should have broken free and killed the dragon herself and not waited while "some crummy old knight" came along. When one of the little boys unwisely attempted to dispute the point, she'd thrown her plasticine at him.

Now she was learning that it wasn't so simple.

It was Helena's nature to decide and act for herself. Her engagement—the one time in her life when she'd been notably indecisive until the last moment—had come about because she

was confused about what she really felt, and wanted. Once her
mind was made up she'd taken clear-cut action, refusing to be
frightened by any thoughts of the consequences.

Now she was forced into a dependence that was foreign to
her. Common sense told her that nothing she could do would
improve matters. The one course of action that lay within her
power—escape—was ruled out by the burden of trust that
Valerio had placed on her. The doors were open, but the
thought of the damage she would do him imprisoned her more
effectively than bolts or bars.

She was powerless to do anything for herself. She could only
sit and wait while her champion fought the battle for her. The
knowledge drove her half-mad with frustration.

She endured it by escaping into her tower—and even this, she
recognized with grim humor, had echoes of the fairy-tale her-
oines that she had despised so much—and painting from dawn
till dusk. It became what Valerio had always intended it to be,
a refuge. At lunchtime Nina would bring up a tray. At other
times she was not disturbed.

She seldom stopped painting to eat, spending the lunch hour
with a brush in one hand and a sandwich in the other. She was
drunk with the joy of rediscovery. She'd almost forgotten how
tiring painting could be and she hurled paint at canvas until her
arms ached, but she couldn't stop.

For the first few days she knew she did badly. She seemed to
have forgotten everything she'd ever known. But suddenly it all
came rushing back. The brush became an extension of her fingers, so that the thoughts seemed to flow down her arm and
straight onto the canvas without a pause.

She was prodigal with canvases. Her painting was a series of
experiments in recapturing her old skill, and as each experi-
ment succeeded she abandoned the canvas she was working on,
and began something new. She felt no guilt about this. She was
like an actress having endless rehearsals before starting work on
the final performance.

The one thing she never tried to paint was a face. She knew
that Valerio's features would haunt any portrait—not, as Maria
believed, out of guilt, but for another reason. Some day soon

she knew she was going to have to face that reason, but for the moment she wasn't ready. So she avoided faces, hoping by this means to blot out the truth.

Just the same, she found herself counting the days till the fortnight would be up. It was painful to know that so much time had to pass before she could hope to see him again. As for what would happen when this was over and their paths would separate forever, she didn't dare allow herself to think of that.

She always made a conscientious effort to go down for dinner. Serena had left for her holiday and Maria frequently dined in her room. After her outburst she'd made no further effort to speak to Helena. So Helena often found herself dining with only Adele for company. These evenings were enjoyable, for there was a real affinity between them. Adele was also, in some ways, an outsider in Florence, although she had lived in the city for sixty years.

"I read those books about the family that you are now reading," she told Helena. "I thought they would give me the key, and in part they did."

"Yes, I hoped they might help me understand Valerio a bit better," Helena agreed.

"It is very simple to understand Valerio," said Adele. "He is a good man. The matter is not complicated at all. But you do not recognize him for what he is, because there are so few good men in the world now."

"I remember him telling me how he gave up his own desire to be an art dealer after his brother died in the floods," said Helena. "I thought then that it was like talking to a man from another century. People don't do that sort of thing anymore."

"Here they do," said Adele. "I don't just mean in Italy. I mean in Florence. This city is not like the rest of the country."

Helena nodded. She'd already sensed this in a vague, indefinable way. When she was fifteen her father had brought her to Italy. They had spent a week in Rome, then one in Venice. It was only in years afterward, when she could set Florence against the other two cities in her mind, that she gained an insight into where the difference lay.

The English say "Florence," a flowing, deceptively musical sound. But the Italians say "Firenze," the tart, acerbic syllables clashing against each other, and bringing the speaker up short at the end of the word. The city does not have the lush, sensuous femininity of Venice, or the Rabelaisian geniality of Rome. Its fame has come from art, but its prosperity has always been based on business.

For centuries, Florence governed itself as a republic, and even the Medici, the nearest to a royal house that the city ever had, only assumed semi-princely status because it was good for their banking business. Lawyers, bankers, statesmen—these, as much as artists, have created the spirit of Florence. And Valerio came from a family steeped in that proud, austere tradition. Several times he had emphasized to Helena that he was Italian, but the truth was that Valerio—poised, elegant, hardheaded—was Florentine to his fingertips.

"I am a Roman," said Adele. "When I first came to Florence I hated it. A woman cannot feel at home here. It is a city of men, and it concerns itself with the business of men. Who are the great artists of Florence? Michelangelo and Leonardo da Vinci, both of whom shut women out of their lives. Who is the greatest poet? Dante, who gave his love to a woman he was careful to keep at a distance.

"This is a cold, hard city, full of cold, hard men. My husband was one such, and Valerio is like him. I thought then that this was very dreadful, but later I began to understand that there is another side. When we had been married for ten years I became ill. I screamed and raged at my husband. If the poor man opened his mouth I let loose a tirade against him, and for a year I kept him out of my bed.

"He bore it like a saint. Never did he speak a word to me that was not gentle, and every evening and every night he was at home. When it was all over I asked him why he had not sought the beds of other women, and he looked at me in bewilderment and said, 'Because I am married to *you*!'

"There is a terrible fidelity about these men, Helena, a fidelity of iron. They cannot make pretty speeches or gestures, but they are the men about whom love songs are written, just the same. Because they love only once. They can love deeply, but not widely. Their whole capacity for love becomes used up in one woman, and after that they are a desert.''

"Adele, I know what you are saying, and you mustn't think this way," Helena pleaded. "The past is over for Valerio and me.''

"For you perhaps. But for him, never. I know my grandson. He does not have a big, warm heart to love all the world. It has only this much room." She made a gesture with her hands. "And *all* of that was taken by you. There is no more for anyone else. Since he lost you, he is barren. I do not wish him to end his life like that.''

Helena shook her head. "He isn't doing this for love. He's doing it because he believes it's right, and because he wants to get rid of me.''

"Right!" said Adele scornfully. "A man with an overgrown conscience is always a fool, or at any rate, he behaves like one, which amounts to the same thing.''

"I've always found Valerio's sense of duty a bit awesome," said Helena reflectively. "It's so rigid and unbending. Otherwise..." she hesitated.

"Otherwise?" Adele prompted hopefully.

"Well, there's something that's always puzzled me. When Valerio and I broke up, ten years ago, I sent him a letter. I explained everything and told him how much I still loved him. I begged him to understand and forgive me. But it was no use. I got the letter back unopened. At least, that's how it looked. But the back of the envelope had that crinkly look that you see when a letter's been steamed open and then sealed up again. If it had been any other man but Valerio I might have thought that he *had* read it, but wanted to pretend he hadn't. But I can't imagine him doing that. If he'd read the letter he'd have admitted it.''

Adele gave a big, guilty smile. "It was me," she said mournfully. "I opened your letter, Helena, and then sealed it up again.''

"You?"

"When it arrived I urged Valerio to open it. I had liked you very much, both for yourself and for the way you'd transformed my stiff, correct grandson into a smiling, happy man. Despite what had happened I believed it was not too late. I thought there had been some misunderstanding between you and it could be put right. You must remember that I'd met you only a couple of times. I didn't know what was really troubling you."

She sighed again. "I couldn't make Valerio listen to me. He forbade anyone to speak your name. It was terrible to see him. But I don't give up easily. I managed to get hold of the letter when he wasn't there. I steamed it open, and when I had read it I resealed it and put it back. Don't be angry with me for this, Helena, I beg you. I wanted only to help. I thought if I knew your reasons I could speak for you more eloquently, and make him soften toward you."

"I'm not angry," said Helena. "But I'm beginning to understand why St. Peter is afraid of you. Valerio once said that the only time he was scared of you was when you were determined to do something for his own good." She gave a wry laugh. "It obviously wasn't any use, though."

"No," confirmed Adele. "When I read your words I thought there must be a chance. It was so obviously all his fault."

Helena looked at her quickly and Adele repeated, "*All* his fault. What was the silly boy thinking of to rush you into marriage when you felt like that? You were a child. He had no right to try to sweep you off your feet without giving you time to think. But so it is with extremely clever men. When they are very much in love, all their cleverness seems to desert them.

"It was so clear to me that you loved him, and that you would have married him in the end, if only he had been patient. Ai-ai-ai- if you could have seen me then. I worked out a clever way to say all this to him without letting him suspect what I had done. And in the end all my cleverness was wasted. At the first mention of your name he left the room.

"He had become as I had never seen him. He had always been a firm man, one who did not forgive easily, but now he was hard and pitiless. I believe the temptation to read your letter tormented him for many weeks, which was why he kept it so long. But in the end he yielded to the cruelty that was now a part of his nature.

"It is only in recent years that I have begun to hope that he has mellowed," Adele went on. "There have been small signs...."

"You mean—" Helena could hardly breathe "—has he ever mentioned me?"

"Not directly, but you are still there. Did Serena tell you that it was Valerio who argued for her being allowed to have the career she wanted?"

"Yes, she did mention it. I thought it strange."

"Not so strange. Maria was very much against it. She said to Valerio, 'Serena will turn into a hard woman, like that one you brought here. Do you want some other man to suffer as you did?' Valerio became very pale, but he only said, 'It is Serena's suffering that concerns me. Neither one of us has the right to decide her life for her.'"

Helena was silent, her heart heavy. Against all reason she had hoped for some unmistakable sign that her memory had softened Valerio's attitude. She knew Adele interpreted the story that way, and perhaps she was right. But it was just as likely that Valerio's affection for his sister, and his strict sense of justice, were the real reasons.

She didn't speak again until they were taking coffee on the terrace. "At least you've cleared up a mystery that was puzzling me," she said at last. "Now I know why you offered to help me, and why you've been on my side."

Adele nodded. "I think a wrong was done to you ten years ago. This family owes you something."

"I don't think anyone owes me anything," insisted Helena. "I made my own decision and it's for me to take the consequences. But I'm afraid Valerio thinks he has a duty toward me, and discharging it is what he cares most about."

After that, to her relief, Adele allowed the subject to drop and they talked about indifferent things, sipped their coffee, then both turned in for an early night.

Nine

Three days later Helena's money arrived from England and she heaved a sigh of relief. She knew she must conserve most of it, but for the moment she had some independence.

Chief on her list of urgent purchases was a new handbag. Her old one had suffered in the accident and was barely holding together. As soon as possible she planned a visit to the Straw Market.

This was situated in the Mercato Nuovo, the four-sided loggia built in the sixteenth century to accommodate the money changers, merchants, silk and wool weavers. After four centuries it was still a marketplace, filled with stalls selling straw hats, pictures, leather goods, chess sets, decorative papier-mâché trays, souvenirs and knickknacks.

There were no walls. The roof was held up by three huge arches on each side. At one end was the large brass boar, known as "Il Porcellino," with its nose shiny where thousands of people had rubbed it and thrown a coin through the grill for the local orphanage.

She had passed the market often with Valerio, for it was situated in the same part of the city as his apartment. Once, wishing to buy him a present, she had taken him to look for a new wallet, and he had shown her the round white stone in the very center of the loggia.

"In the sixteenth century when this place was built," he'd said, "that spot was known as the Place of Shame. Merchants who'd been found out in fraudulent dealings were made to stand there, exposed to public scorn."

The day after her money arrived Helena prepared to go to town, and waited for Giorgio to pick her up. But there was no sign of him and after a while she went down to the little cottage on the grounds where he lived with his wife Dora. There she found Giorgio sitting in trousers and vest, his hair rumpled, looking as though he'd just got up.

"One moment," he promised, "one moment, then I am with you."

Dora sniffed, "One moment? Huh! The state you came home in last night! I tell you it will be tomorrow before you are useful for anything." She bustled away, muttering. "And even then, not *very* useful."

Helena laughed. "Hung over?" she said sympathetically. A groan was the only response. Giorgio was definitely the worse for wear.

"Look," she said suddenly, "you stay here. I can get into town by myself."

"My orders are to go with you, always," he said miserably.

"But you're not fit to drive," she pointed out. "I'll be safer without you than with you."

This was indisputably true and Giorgio scratched his head unhappily. "Signor Lucci will not like it," he said at last.

"Signor Lucci will never know," she promised. "He's not due back for another four days." It occurred to her that this would also free her from the danger of bumping into him accidentally. If ever she was going to play hooky this was her chance. "Look, nothing's happened to me when I've gone off on my own before, and nothing's going to happen now," she assured him. "Don't worry about me. I'll look in on you when I get back. Now I'm off!"

She was out the door before Giorgio could think of anything to say. She felt lighthearted at the prospect of a few hours of freedom. In a few moments she was out of the gate and walking swiftly down the hill. At the bottom she hailed a taxi and gave the driver the address of the police station, for she wanted to make her daily report before she did anything else.

At the police station she found Sergeant Torrini on duty. She knew him from previous visits, and recognized him as the man she'd seen soothing Guido Ranelli in the court. Something in his manner then had given her the impression that the two were friendly. Perhaps because of this she had always felt she detected a faint hostility in his attitude toward her, but this, she realized, might be no more than her imagination. His way of speaking to her was always impeccably polite.

"Good morning, *signora*," he said as she approached the desk. "You are on time as always." He reached into the desk and pulled out the book that she had to sign. While she was doing so he looked around, then at the door. "Giorgio does not come in with you this morning?" he said.

"He isn't with me," she said abstractedly as she finished the signature and pushed it across for him to sign in confirmation that he had seen her.

"Not with you? You mean not at all?" Sergeant Torrini didn't look at her. His whole attention seemed to be given to writing, and there was nothing in his voice to suggest that he cared for her answer one way or another.

"No, I left him behind today. I want to do some shopping and it would only bore him."

"You mean that you are completely alone?" The sergeant stamped the book with a large rubber date stamp.

"Yes. Well why not? The order said I had to report here. It didn't say I had to have an escort." She was beginning to feel a little cross. "Why shouldn't I have a day out on my own?"

"There is no reason at all, *signora*," he said with a bland smile. "I hope you enjoy your shopping expedition."

He stood watching her as she walked out of the station, the smile fixed to his face. Only when he was quite sure she was gone did he snatch up the telephone and bark into it, "Get me a line—quickly!"

It took Helena only half an hour in the Straw Market to equip herself with a new handbag, belt and shoes. As she departed she rubbed the nose of Il Porcellino, pushed her coin through the grill, then went off in search of a coffee bar.

She found one almost immediately. When she'd given her order to the waiter she pulled out her purchases to examine them. She was pleased with all of them, and she felt she'd gotten a genuine bargain with the purse. With some minor modifications from her clever fingers it could be made to look really original. She was turning it over in her hands, planning what she would do to it, when a man seated himself opposite her. Looking up she found the hard eyes of Guido Ranelli fixed on her.

"You have no objection if I sit here, *signora*?" he said.

"Of course not." There was nothing else to say. She wasn't afraid of Ranelli, and she wasn't going to give him the impression that she was.

"Of course not." His mouth stretched in a smile as he softly mimicked her, but the smile did not reach his eyes. "Of course not. Why should you object? Almost one might think that you did not know who I was?"

"I know who you are," she said, determined to carry the war into his territory. "You are Guido Ranelli, Lucilla Dorani's fiancé. I saw you in court."

He raised one eyebrow satirically. "You saw me in court?" he repeated quietly. "Of course you did. And you heard me too, did you not? Or perhaps my words did not reach you clearly? Shall I repeat them to you now?"

"There's no need," she said. "I heard you. I understand why you blame me, but—"

"Oh, you understand?" he interrupted her. "Well, that is very helpful, *signora*, because maybe you also understand why

I hate you, why I would be glad to see you smashed and helpless as my Lucilla is this moment.''

There was no change in his tone as he said this. It was quiet,
level, almost friendly. A stranger, watching them, would have
concluded that they were talking amicably. Only she could see
the stony look in Ranelli's eyes, and hear the chill undertone of
menace in his voice. But she refused to let him intimidate her,
and her voice was steady as she said, ''I was going to say that
you have no cause to blame me. I wasn't drunk that night.''

''Oh, you have remembered what happened then? How
strange that no news of this has reached my ears. I am, as you
may imagine, keeping myself fully informed of everything you
do. I have more friends in this city than you have, *signora*. They
tell me what I want to know. I am aware of every occasion that
you have given Giorgio the slip. It was only a matter of time
before you were so foolish as to leave him behind altogether.''

He gave an almost inaudible laugh, and Helena began to feel
sick. She had walked into a trap that had been laid a long time
before. Valerio had tried to warn her and she had refused to
listen. Now Valerio was a long way off, and she would have to
take care of herself.

''So now tell me,'' Ranelli went on, leaning toward her with
an air of friendly interest, ''tell me what really happened that
night, since you have evidently remembered everything.''

''I haven't remembered,'' she said. ''I didn't mean that.''

''You didn't mean that. You haven't remembered,'' he
intoned.

''Is it necessary to repeat everything I say?'' she snapped, and
he laughed out loud. She could have kicked herself for betray-
ing her tension. Of course Ranelli was trying to wear her down
with this repetition that was like the Chinese water torture, and
now he knew that he was succeeding.

''So,'' he said with a shrug, ''we are back to the old plea of
amnesia. You managed to deceive the court, with the help of
the man you are making a fool of, but you aren't deceiving me.
I don't believe in your convenient amnesia. I don't care whether
you were drunk or Hanley was drunk. What does it matter?
You are two of a kind. You went to a party that no decent

woman would go to, a party given by a—'' He used a filthy word.

''I didn't know what kind of man Santi was,'' she said.

''You are a liar,'' said Ranelli with an indifferent shrug. ''It is no more than I expected, but please don't waste my time with denials. It only makes me angry.''

''I'm not lying,'' she said fiercely. ''How could I know about Santi? I barely set eyes on him when I met him at the fair. And what about Lucilla? She was at that party too, remember? She lives in Florence. She must know more about him than I do. Isn't she a decent wo—''

The last word became a cry of pain as he took her hand and crushed it sharply in his big one. Now his eyes were glittering. ''Do not,'' he said with soft venom, ''dare to say such a thing. You are not fit to speak her name. She is an innocent child.''

''Then it's a pity you didn't take better care of her,'' she flashed. He had released her hand now but it still hurt. She dropped it below the table so that he didn't have the satisfaction of seeing her flex the fingers.

''I forbade her to go near Santi's house,'' he said broodingly. ''But I had to be away that night, and it didn't occur to me that she would ignore my wishes. But she did. She went in the company of a man whose name I have since learned. He abandoned her, leaving her to your mercies, and you nearly killed her. I have dealt with him. It remains only for me to deal with you.''

''I've heard enough,'' she said angrily. ''I don't believe I've done wrong, but if I have, the court will say so. I'm not going to sit here any longer listening to idiotic threats, which don't frighten me. I'm sorry for you, Signor Ranelli, but you are wasting your time.''

Her heart was thumping as she said these words, giving the lie to her assertion that she wasn't afraid. But pride kept her head up and her voice steady. She called the waiter and paid her bill, all the time anticipating a movement from Ranelli to prevent her. But there was none. He just sat there, regarding her with an amused smile that never wavered, and that unnerved her more than his threats had done. Finally she got to her feet and pushed past him. Every nerve in her body was quivering with anticipation, and she sensed the moment he rose and followed her out of the coffee bar. But she did not turn her head to give him so much as one look.

She could hear his footsteps just behind her, dogging hers so closely that once she stumbled. And all the time he talked in that terrifying low voice that managed to be perfectly audible, and went on and on....

"You are afraid of me whether you admit it or not, *signora*. That is why you run away. And you are right to be afraid. I have thought for a long time of what I would do if this moment ever arrived. The long-planned revenge is always the best, is it not? It is more refined, and it is the refinements that give pleasure, as you will discover...."

If he didn't shut up she'd start screaming. The thundering of her heart seemed to fill the world, but it couldn't blot out the sound of that terrifying voice. Once she increased her pace, but he immediately did the same, so that they collided slightly and she stumbled again. This time he caught hold of her to steady her. She pulled away and he let her go easily.

"It's all right," he said in a soothing tone. "There's no hurry. You're going in the direction I want you to take."

"The direction you...?"

"But of course! Why do you think I let you leave? If I'd wanted you to stay, you would have stayed. But we were about to leave together, I assure you. You just made it easy for me. No, not that way—" He darted in front of her as she turned away. "Just keep going the way you were. I'll tell you when we get there."

It was like a nightmare in which she was running and running, but her limbs were like lead and she hardly moved. She'd believed herself to be escaping Ranelli. Now she discovered that she was only walking further into his trap. She had not the least doubt that what he said was true. The spider had planned this long ago, and sat laughing as the fly walked blindly into his web.

Then she saw what she'd been frantically seeking, a taxi. It appeared a few yards ahead and slowed in answer to her cry.

She began to run, breathing a fervent prayer of relief that she had been saved.

But Ranelli was running with her, keeping up easily. She tried to tell herself that it didn't matter. The taxi driver would help her. But when she was a few feet away Ranelli's arm snaked around her waist and caught her against him in a firm grip. She gasped and began to struggle, but he had both arms around her, one hand cradling her head, holding it firm so that she couldn't turn it. Her cry for help was cut off by the pressure of his mouth on hers.

She tried to fight him, revolted by the feel of the unwanted embrace. The smell of his flesh assailed her nostrils, making her gag, but there was no relief. His grip constrained her so that she couldn't struggle properly, and the vehemence of her resistance was concealed. Passersby saw only two lovers making up after a tiff, the girl a little unwilling perhaps, but the man standing no nonsense. The taxi driver grinned and drove on.

At last Ranelli took his mouth from hers and laughed fiercely into her face. "No one will help you against me, *signora*. Try it!"

She opened her mouth to scream and was immediately smothered again in the same way as last time. This time he kept up the pressure until she was half suffocating, and when he drew his mouth away her head was spinning. She was filled with despair. She didn't dare try to scream again, lest he silence her in the same way.

He was moving, half dragging, half carrying her along the street with him. She looked around frantically, wondering where he was taking her. At last the Straw Market came into view, the sun shining on the polished nose of Il Porcellino.

"We're nearly there," said Ranelli's voice in her ear. "Just a few yards farther."

Then she knew where he was taking her and why, and she started to struggle desperately. Now passersby began to realize that something was wrong. Some of them stared, some called out, but none was sufficiently sure what was happening to intervene. Ranelli abandoned the loverlike pose and began to walk faster, overcoming her struggles with a grip of iron.

He reached the edge of the market and dragged her up the steps and through the crowd. In a few seconds he had reached the round white slab in the center and forced her down to her knees with a violence that jarred through her. With his left hand he took a firm, painful grip on her hair. With his right he pulled out a knife and jabbed it toward the crowd converging on him. They backed away hastily.

"I use this on the first man who troubles me before I am finished," he threatened. "What I have to say will not take long, but I will say it and no one shall stop me. I have brought this woman here to the Place of Shame because the courts will not punish her for what she has done, and so I must. If the law denies me vengeance I must take it for myself. *Look at her!*"

He jerked the hand behind Helena's head, forcing it back even farther than before. Tears started from her eyes and fell helplessly down her cheeks. The downward pull kept her on her knees and her face was exposed to the crowd, who were staring at her curiously.

"Look at her," repeated Ranelli. "This is the woman who butchered my Lucilla, and she thinks she will go free while the innocent girl she destroyed with her drunkenness and stupidity will never be the same again. *Well, I say no!*" His voice rose to a scream. *"I say she shall suffer for what she has done. I say—"*

His next word was choked off as though someone had thrust it back down his throat. Helena felt one last painful yank on her hair, then it was released suddenly and she fell sideways. The world was swimming but she forced herself up. As soon as she reached her feet her legs gave way again. Hands reached out to pull her back out of the path of what she now realized were two men fighting.

Then suddenly it was all over. Ranelli was on the ground, blood pouring down his chin, his eyes burning with hate. Standing over him, his shirt torn, his face cut, was Valerio.

Valerio looked around the crowd, his face full of contempt. "You call yourselves men? Not one of you could find the guts to save a woman. I tell you, every one of you is a disgrace."

There is no greater insult one Italian can offer another than to call him a disgrace, and there were murmurs of anger from the men in the crowd. But nothing further happened. The memory of how Valerio had disarmed and overcome a man with a knife was too recent for anyone to feel like taking him on.

Valerio turned to Helena and took her by the arm. He didn't dignify Ranelli with so much as a look as he led her out of the crowd. Helena kept her chin determinedly up as she walked beside him. She knew that her face was streaked with tears, her tights torn and her knees grazed, but she carried her head high, and met every curious stare she encountered.

As they left the market, Valerio said curtly, "My car is just over here." He led her the short distance, keeping hold of her arm. When she was installed in the passenger seat he got in beside her and swung the car away.

She wanted to ask him a thousand questions—how he had come to be here when she had thought him many miles away, how he had known of her plight. Above all she wanted to ask him if he was hurt. But even from the side she could see that Valerio's expression was one of bleak grimness that discouraged questions.

After a few moments he stopped the car and she looked out. Until then she'd hardly given a thought to where he was taking her, but now she realized that they were in the winding street where he had his apartment.

He grasped her hand to help her out of the car. Another second and she was through the front door and climbing the stairs to the second floor, to be confronted by the door of Valerio's apartment—a door she had last seen ten years ago, when she had beaten her hands raw against its unyielding surface.

She went slowly in ahead of him. Now that she was no longer in the public gaze she felt the strength and energy flowing out of her and reaction setting in. She was shivering, but she tried to force herself to be steady as she turned to face him. She still had the ordeal of Valerio's wrath to get through, and there was no way she could blame him for his anger.

But there was no anger in his eyes as he stood looking at her. His face was confused and disbelieving, as though he had received a stunning blow. "I promised myself that you would never be allowed in here again," he said in an unsteady voice, "but that was a long time ago. When I saw him hurting you I wanted to kill him. Helena—*oh, my God!*"

She didn't see him reach for her. She only felt his arms go around her, pulling her hard against himself. As if by some knowledge of their own her arms found their old place round his neck. Her hand fitted the curve of his head, pressing him close. They did not kiss, but stood for a long time in each other's embrace, feeling the pain and bitterness of years dissolve in the sweetness of reconciliation. They needed no words to tell them that they had found each other again.

It had been such a long, desolate time since she had known the joy of his arms about her. Now they were strong and tender, and held her close in protection and comfort.

"He might have killed you," she said with a shudder. "He had a knife." She touched Valerio's cheek where the cut was bleeding. "Did he do this?"

"I don't know. Perhaps. It doesn't matter." His words became lost in a murmur as he began to rain soft kisses on her face. But there was no passion in them. Each kiss was a consoling caress to soothe away her pain, and she gave herself up to the happiness, too exhausted to do more than rest.

At last he realized the state she was in and lifted her in his arms. She was carried the few feet to the bedroom and laid gently on the bed. As soon as he set her down his arms were around her again, holding her close to his heart in a long, silent moment, while the world seemed to stop.

"Why?" he said at last. "For God's sake, tell me why you did anything so stupid, after I'd warned you?"

"I thought you were just being overcautious. I never saw him before."

"He's been biding his time."

"Yes, he told me. I couldn't believe it, that anyone should be so calculatedly vicious and vindictive—"

"We are a cruel people, Helena," he said somberly. "We show a sunny face to the world, but beneath it we are violent and bloodthirsty. Luckily for you I'm as violent as he."

"How did you get there? I thought you were still away on holiday."

"I was away but it wasn't really a holiday—more like an escape. You know why. I knew you were dangerous to me and I needed to put some distance between us. But I'd left it until too late. I couldn't stop thinking about you, and as I did, I became afraid. I know how headstrong you can be, and how you refuse to be told anything. You'd never believe anything was dangerous until you'd tried it for yourself and got hurt. I thought it would be just like you to do something reckless the minute my back was turned. And you did.

"I got back last night. I was going to come and see you this morning and I was on the verge of calling the villa when the phone rang. Luckily for you, Sergeant Torrini is a conscientious man. He'd rung my office to warn me that you were on your own. My secretary knew I was back, and she called me here to pass on the message. I tore out of this place and drove around looking for you. In the end I only found you because of the commotion."

"Sergeant Torrini warned you?" Helena said in wonder. "I always had the feeling that he was a friend of Ranelli's."

"He is. That's how he knew you were in danger. He's a good policeman and he didn't want any trouble. Also, I think he was trying to protect Ranelli from the consequences of his own craziness."

"Yes, he is crazy," she said and shuddered. "It was like trying to talk to a madman. I didn't know what he was going to do and I got more and more scared. I couldn't get rid of him, and then—" She stopped and closed her eyes.

"Tell me," he said quietly. "Tell me and I'll make it go away."

"When we got into the street I tried to run for the taxi, but he grabbed me and kissed me so I wouldn't scream. No one would help me..." Now she couldn't hold back the tears as the remembered horror swept over her. The loathsome feel of Ranelli's cruel mouth was still on hers.

"I can't get rid of him," she sobbed. "I know I'll never forget and he'll always be there."

"Hush," he said. "Trust me."

He raised her wet face and stroked it with tender fingers. Then he bent his head, and the lips she had longed for touched hers again. He kissed her gently so as not to hurt her bruised flesh, but there was authority in every movement, as though he was giving her a wordless command to forget all men but him. She obeyed it eagerly, giving herself up to the sweet, remembered sensation of belonging to him.

Her lips fell apart at the first urging of his tongue. At first she was aware only of contentment, the blissful feeling that Valerio had once more opened his arms to her. But gradually the old flames, which he could fan her life with the lightest breath, began to flicker through her. His mouth moved against hers as he took possession, tracing a leisurely path around the soft inside, rediscovering the warmth and sweetness he had loved.

She moaned softly at the sensations that were surging through her, and reached out to hold him as he drew back. She was afraid that he meant only to kiss her, to wipe away Ranelli, and then let her go. But when she saw his face she knew she had nothing to fear. His breath was coming unevenly and there was a haggard look on his face. The unfulfilled passion of ten years had him in its grip, and there was no turning back now, for him or for her.

"You are mine," he said. "You have always belonged to me, from the first moment. Even when you were married to another man, you were always mine, never his. Now, you have returned to me."

"I'm dreaming," she said in wonder. "I dreamed so often that I hadn't really gone away, that it was all something that happened in a bad dream, and I would wake to find myself here in your arms. But then I really woke, and you weren't there, and the bad dream was my life after all."

"It is no dream," he said. "We were always meant to find each other again. Now we have done so, heart of my heart. Come to me. We have wasted so many years."

At once she clasped her hands behind his head and pulled him down to her. Her mouth was ready for his, eagerly seeking him, open to his welcome invasion. The old sensation was still there, the pressure of his lips on hers, that no other man had been able to obliterate. Then his tongue claimed her, teased and challenged the inside of her mouth till she moaned with torment and anticipation.

He began to undress her with feverish hands, never taking his mouth from hers. He fumbled over her dress and she helped him, anxious for the moment when she would be naked in his arms.

When she was wearing only her bra and panties she stopped him and reached for his clothes. Once, long ago, he had laughed at her when she began to pull open his buttons, delighting in her shameless eagerness to make love to him. Now he watched her with wary eyes, as though troubled by something he could not share with her. But he let her do as she wished and in a moment his chest was bare. At once she leaned forward and kissed him at the base of the throat, as he had loved.

A shudder went through him at the touch of her lips. He removed her bra with swift, urgent movements and pulled her against him, groaning as he felt the hard nipples against his chest.

At once Helena sensed the change in him. His tenderness had become swamped by a primitive masculine urge to possess. The hands that roved over her were ungentle, as long pent-up desire took control of him. Her panties were stripped from her in a second. She couldn't have stopped him now if she'd wanted to. But she didn't want to. Her body was alive and singing with expectation for the first time in years. She had been made for this man's loving, and no other. She was back where she belonged.

His clothes followed hers onto the floor, and she was in his arms again, feeling her flesh vibrating to the demands of his.

His weight pressed down on her; he was there between her thighs, seeking the place he knew, where he would pierce the heart of her passion. She offered herself gladly to his conquest and cried out when the moment came, for the sweet-sharp ecstasy was almost unendurable. His own fulfillment came almost at once and his cry mingled with hers.

It was the briefest and most violent union they had ever had. They'd wanted each other too long to linger over subtleties, and now they were left breathing hard, each reeling from the shock of rediscovery, staring at each other with new eyes.

"I didn't mean to be like that," he said abruptly. "Did I hurt you?"

She shook her head, unable to speak, her eyes still fixed on him. At last her breathing subsided and her blood slowed its mad race. Valerio too was calmer, though still aroused, as she could see. He reached out and touched her in the old gentle way.

"I couldn't help myself," he said. "I never could help myself where you were concerned. I swore a thousand times that this wouldn't happen. And all the time I knew that I was only trying to convince myself. Whenever we were alone, you were never safe for one minute."

"I never wanted to be safe," she breathed. "I only wanted to reach out to you, but I thought you despised me."

She thought he said "Never!" but the word was muffled as he dropped his head to rest his lips against the fullness of her breast. After a long moment he lifted it again, but his eyes remained fixed on her length.

"You have changed," he said slowly. "You are rounder and more generously formed. You left me a child, you have come back a woman. And yet you are still just as my heart remembered."

"How have I changed?" she said, longing to know how she looked in his eyes, and also wanting to keep his attention just where it was.

"Here..." He placed one long finger on the curve of her breast and let it drift lazily over the swell and down again till he could cup the fullness in his hand. She stretched in languorous delight, careful not to move out of his palm.

It seemed almost accidental that his thumb rasped across the nipple as his hand slid lower. But Helena knew it was no accident. Nor were the lazy circles he was tracing on her stomach, setting off tremors in her loins.

"And here..." he went on, stroking the generous curve of her hip, and letting his hand linger a moment before drawing it down her thigh. "How often have I sat and watched you across the dinner table, trying to imagine how you would look without your clothes, and hurting inside because at one time I wouldn't have had to imagine. And there was an added pain in the thought that any other man had seen you like this, when you belonged to me."

"Valerio, listen to me," she said urgently, raising herself above him and taking his face between her hands. "There's been no one since I left my husband. *No one at all!* You must believe that."

He turned his head so that his lips were against her palm. "I do believe it, now," he said. His arms wove around her back, keeping her against him. "I've been through hell wondering about Hanley, but I knew as soon as I held you that there were no ghosts there."

"What about my husband?" she said, hardly daring to say the words. "Is he a ghost?"

He scowled. "It's better if you don't ask me to think about him. I feel almost as if you were my wife and you'd— Well, no matter. I'm not being fair. You were his wife, not mine." But his face was drawn with pain as he spoke.

"Was that what was troubling you?" she said. "You were frowning."

"Partly that. Perhaps it sounds silly, but I was afraid you were going to change your mind at the last moment. So I didn't give you the chance."

He smiled faintly on the last words, but she realized that he was actually deadly serious. The old rejection, the fact that it seemed as though she had publicly scorned him after he had been her lover—these still wounded him deeply.

Now Helena knew what she had to do. In the past she had told herself that the events of their wedding day had been his fault as much as hers. But that no longer counted. She was a woman, and she had a woman's ability to discount irrelevancies, such as who was to blame, and to think only of the thing that mattered: she loved this man, he was hurt and only she could ease his pain.

Her hand still lay against his face. She let it slide lower to find the base of his throat, drawing her fingertips lightly across the tender place. She felt the faintest tremor communicate itself from him to her through the palm of her hand as it slid over his chest. She had pulled back a little to enjoy the sight of his magnificent naked length, powerful with muscles where before there had been only lean wiriness. His eyes were watching her intently, but the change in his breathing told her that he was acutely aware of her intentions.

Her body ached with desire as if the past few minutes had never been, and dropping her eyes, she saw that it was the same with him. He was totally aroused, but he did not move. He simply waited and let her make love to him, his lips curved in a grave, gentle smile.

Her fingers still lay against his chest. She flexed them so that the nails grazed lightly against his skin. She did this again and again, knowing she was straining his self-control to the utmost. She leaned across and would have dropped her head to let her lips take up the work of her hands, but he stopped her with a tense grasp on her shoulder.

"Helena, don't do this unless you really mean it," he said in a hoarse voice.

"I mean it, my love, my lover."

"But why?"

"I'm doing what I've wanted to do every minute since we parted. I've ached for you; nothing ever blotted you out. You were always there in my mind, in my heart. I shouldn't have gone away from your door that day. I should have stayed there until you opened up to me—forever if necessary. I'd have *made* you forgive me!"

"I knew that. That was why I shut you out. I knew I'd never be able to resist you if I saw you. But at the same time I was afraid I might kill you before I forgave you. My hate was as violent as my love. When I think of what I threw away in pride and anger—"

Her mouth silenced him. Then she was raining kisses over his face, his neck, while her hands caressed him luxuriously, seeking the familiar places that they had loved to touch. She played the siren shamelessly, trying by every means in her power to let him know that she desired him, that all the riches of her body were his to command and that all she wanted in the world was to feel him inside her and to show him how much he pleased her.

She felt him turn suddenly and press her down into the bed. Her legs parted for him and at once he possessed her with one long, slow movement that sent her into a spin of delight, then another and another as he claimed and reclaimed her with leisurely power. She gave a low moan and felt it smothered by his lips against hers, murmuring, "You're mine...always... mine...."

"Yes," she whispered, half out of her mind with the long-drawned-out poignancy of every movement.

"You belong to me. Let me hear you say it...."

She moved her lips soundlessly, but he seemed satisfied, for he smiled at her, his face brilliant with joy as it had been once before in this same room, at their first loving. Happiness swamped her. Whatever else happened in their lives, she would always know that she had given him this one moment when he had been like a god again.

His movements became more forceful, his rhythm increasing until she cried out, feeling herself spinning away into nothingness, lost in the shattering awareness of total union, total fulfillment. Her hands raked his back as she gave herself up to him in a surrender that was absolute and she knew that she had come home.

It was over, but he did not release her. Instead he kept her cradled in his arms, watching her with tender loving eyes while bliss and contentment suffused her, until at last she fell asleep.

She was in a dark place. There was noise all around her, and the atmosphere filled her with dread. From somewhere nearby she could hear a tearful, pleading voice. Brian was there, laughing like a madman, but angry too, saying "Don't make such a fuss!"

She woke to find Valerio sitting beside her, shaking her gently.

"You were having a nightmare," he said. "You kept saying 'I've got to make a fuss, I've got to make a fuss' over and over again. You sounded quite desperate. Who were you talking to?"

"Brian," she said. "It's come back to me. I know what happened."

Ten

For a moment Valerio stared at her, without moving. Then he pulled her up and took hold of her shoulders, studying her face eagerly.

"Quickly," he said. "Tell me everything before you forget."

She shook her head to clear it. "You were right," she said after a moment. "I hardly had anything to drink at all. It was Brian; he was in a terrible state. When it was time to leave, I tried to persuade him not to go. I was sure Santi would put us up for the night.

"But by that time he'd promised Lucilla we'd take her home. She grew frantic. She said if she stayed out all night Guido would find out and be furious with her. I said someone else should take her home, but a lot of people had already gone. Of the ones who were left I think we were the only ones coming back to Florence. So it had to be us. She begged and pleaded and Brian said we'd take her.

"When I argued, he said, 'Don't make such a fuss.' I said I had to make a fuss, because it was so dangerous. Then he said, 'Why don't you drive if you're so sober?' I said I couldn't, I didn't have my license on me. But then I looked at the way he was weaving about, and I thought perhaps I ought to do it. Only he got into the driver's seat while I was still hesitating, and said 'Come on, or we'll go without you.'

"Lucilla got in the front seat and I got in the back. Brian drove off, but he couldn't control the car. We were swerving back and forth across the road, going down a hill. It was terrifying.

"When we got to the bottom, the road curved suddenly, but the car kept going straight, and we shot right off the road. Luckily there was only a grass verge, and no one was hurt. But after that I decided to drive.

"At first I couldn't move Brian. He just lay there, giggling. But eventually I managed to persuade him to get out of the car and helped him into the back seat, and I took over the driving."

"And the accident," said Valerio urgently. "How did that happen?"

She screwed her face up, trying to remember. But the closer she came to the actual moment of impact the more her memories faded.

"It's no good," she said at last in despair. "I've no idea why I lost control and hit that truck. I guess I was just confused."

"All right. Don't worry about it. You've remembered this much. The rest will come."

But there was a heaviness in his manner that she understood. "It doesn't really help, does it?" she said. "They'll say you gave me the idea at the hearing."

"They'll try. It would help if we could produce an independent witness. Did anyone see you and Hanley arguing about who should drive?"

"No one. When we arrived at the party the grounds were already packed with cars. We had to park on a little side road a short distance away. There were two other cars there at the time, but they left before we did. It was deserted when we came out."

"What about Santi? Didn't he come out with you?"

"He was pretty incapable himself by that time. The last I saw of him he was sprawled on a sofa. His eyes were open but he was staring at the ceiling with an utterly blissful, idiotic expression on his face. It was that sort of party."

"So you have no witnesses to your departure. What's worse, your memory stops short of the vital facts. You were still driving, and you seem to have caused the collision."

"Which means that if Lucilla dies I'll go to prison for manslaughter."

At once his arms were around her, crushing her to him. *"No!"* he said violently. "Before I let that happen I'll tear the prison down with my bare hands. Trust me, beloved. I won't let anything happen to you. I swore that on the first day when I found you weeping in that hospital ward, and I knew that I could not bear to see you hurt. Have I failed you so far?"

"No, never. I do trust you, Valerio. I've never felt that before, that there was someone I could rely on totally. It always seemed safer to rely on myself. Now I can't; I have to leave it all to you, but I'm not afraid."

She wondered at herself for feeling so lighthearted when things were still so black. But the threat of prison had very little reality for her at this moment. What mattered was that Valerio had welcomed her back into his heart. Locked in the safety of his embrace, she cared very little for the outside world.

At that moment her head was on his shoulder, so she was unable to see his eyes, or the shadow that darkened them. "How strange," she mused happily, "that out of all the lawyers in Florence it should be you they sent to me. I never believed in fate before. I thought it was up to everyone to decide their own destiny. Now I'm not so sure."

"I have always had that belief in fate that you lacked," he said. "And I know that it works in many different ways. I believed that you were dead in my heart. I told myself that you must be to me no more than any other client, but it was a delusion, and I think I always knew it.

"But now—" the note in his voice changed suddenly, and he pushed her away a little "—I am going to do what you will think very cruel. I'm going to take you back to the villa, and from now on, we shall see as little of each other as possible."

She stared at him, only half believing that she had heard him correctly.

"Helena, beloved, listen to me," he said urgently, seizing her hands to stop them from going around his neck. "Have you any idea what a disgraceful thing I've done today? I'm in a position of trust with you, exactly as if I were a doctor. Any doctor who behaved as I have would be thrown out. I could be disbarred if it became known."

"Is that it?" she said indignantly. "You're afraid that I'm going to talk and ruin you? Do you trust me so little?"

"I would trust you with my soul. Otherwise I would never have taken the risk of bringing you into my house. I've given you the power to ruin me twice over, by escaping and by exposing my behavior to the world. I wouldn't have given you that power if I did not believe in your honor.

"But, don't you see, it is *I* who have abused *your* trust. You are in my power, virtually my prisoner. Why do you think the judge said it was only my reputation as a man of honor that made him agree? Why do you think he was so emphatic that I shouldn't live in the villa? So that you should be safe from 'attentions' that you were not in a position to refuse."

"I know," she said impatiently, "but that's all academic. You don't force yourself on me, so why do you talk as though you did? You know I wanted you as much as you wanted me, how happy I was..." She could say no more. Disappointment swept achingly through her for there was an implacable look on his face that she knew of old.

"Darling," he pleaded, "try to understand. What I want from you can only be given freely."

"But I did—"

"No you didn't," he said harshly. "How can you give anything freely to a man who holds your fate in his hand? How can you give freely to a man who has just rescued you from your attacker like some cardboard film hero? If the day ever comes when you are strong enough to tell me to go to hell, *then* I shall believe you made a free choice. But no woman as vulnerable as you can do anything freely."

She stared at him in despair and frustration. Theoretically she knew he was correct, but she judged with her heart, not her head. And her heart had a simple directness that made the writhings of Valerio's conscience look like an occupation for bedlam.

"Oh, you and your damned honor!" she cried.

He gave a grim smile. "You've seen precious little of my honor. You always had the power to make me forget it. From the beginning, haven't I always taken advantage of you—of your youth and inexperience? I first brought you to this room, a child of seventeen, who didn't know what she was doing or what she wanted, but who put her hand in mine and followed my lead trustingly."

"But, I thought you loved me—"

"I did love you. That was my only excuse. It was also my excuse for rushing you headlong down a path you weren't ready for. I know how much of what happened was my fault. I should have waited till you were ready for marriage, but I was afraid to wait in case I lost you. I thought I could imprison you within my love, and then you would come to see things my way, as prisoners often do. I was too much in love to see how selfish I was being. So I blundered on—and lost you anyway.

"And afterward, in my pride and arrogance, I shut my door against you to make you pay for the pain you had caused me. But we have both paid, I as much as you. And now today, what have I done? I have taken advantage of your suffering to present myself as a rescuer to whom everything must be given. *Honor!*" He said the last word with profound self-disgust.

"Then why did you do it?" she demanded.

"My excuse now is the same as it was before. You are there in my heart, and you won't go away. You can make me forget all other considerations—for a while. But afterward they return to torment me."

She looked at him sadly. This was less than the wholehearted declaration of love she had hoped for.

"But what about me?" she said. "I love you. Didn't you think of the possibility? What does your conscience have to say about that?"

He took her face between her hands. "You don't know whether you love me or not," he said gently. "You cannot know, any more than the child you were ten years ago could really know. Then you were intoxicated with passion, but not so intoxicated that you couldn't see the dangers more clearly than I. Now you are intoxicated with danger."

She shook her head insistently. "I love you. Why can't you just believe that? It's so simple."

"Not for me. Darling, please try to understand. We don't know what the future may hold. Let's not try to make decisions now."

"But you've just made one," she said stubbornly. "You're going to shut me out."

"For your own sake," he said firmly. "Yes, this is one decision that I have made, and I won't be moved from it."

She knew him when his mouth set in those obstinate lines. There would be no budging him, and she might as well give in. But her heart was heavy because the cup had been dashed from her lips when she had barely tasted it.

Valerio had risen and left her. She began to dress herself. As she did so she noticed details of the room, which was very little changed. There was the brass bedstead that she remembered, although the counterpane was different. Some new pictures hung on the walls, and it seemed to her that Valerio had begun to collect antiques.

When she was dressed she went out into the kitchen, where she found him looking around himself with an unsatisfied air. "Since I got back only yesterday there's hardly any food in the place," he said. "I ate out last night, and today I was going to stock up, but I didn't get the chance. We'll have to find a restaurant."

"Is it safe," she said, "after what you've just said?"

"Perfectly safe. There's no reason why I shouldn't take my client to dine in a public place. It's being alone here I'm determined to avoid in future." He stopped and kissed her quickly. "And you don't need to tell me that I was the one who brought you here. I know it. It was wrong of me, but I can't regret it. Whatever happens in the future, we found each other again."

She clung to him, but after a moment he pushed her firmly away, although she could tell it was an effort for him.

She'd slept longer than she'd realized, for when they stepped out into the empty street it was nearly dark. Valerio led her toward the river. As they reached the bank the floodlit length of the Ponte Vecchio stood out brilliantly in the darkness. He headed toward it and in another moment they were walking between the goldsmiths' shops that lined the old bridge. It had been in one of these very shops that he'd bought their wedding rings, and her diamond engagement ring. She wondered what he'd done with them, and realized that he had probably come straight back here and returned them.

On the other side of the river, Valerio turned immediately and took her into a small restaurant where the light was dim and the tables lit by candles. They settled at a table by the window, and she understood why the room was kept so dark. The window looked out on the river, and as she ate she could still see the floodlit bridge. She stared, entranced by its beauty.

Despite her disappointment at Valerio's resolution, she was still suffused by the afterglow of loving, replete with physical contentment that blurred the world's harsh edges. She looked up to find him smiling at her, his face bathed in the soft, golden light from the candles.

She waited till the waiter had served the first course before saying, "What happened to you? Did you ever start dealing in art?"

"Yes, I do quite well in a small way. Of course I don't have time for much, but it gives me great pleasure."

"Did you finish your course at the academy?"

"I did eventually. At first I refused to go back, because I thought you would be there. I refused even to go near the place. But then I heard you weren't returning to Florence, so I went back to complete my course."

"I went to Paris and finished studying there."

"I know."

"You know? How?"

"Five years ago you exhibited some pictures in the Young British Artists exhibition in London. It was described in an international art magazine I subscribed to, and there was a brief biography of you. So I know quite a bit about you. I know you took the hitchhiking trip you told me about, with your paints and easel."

She made a face. "It was all a big mistake, that trip. I don't know why, but it just didn't work."

"You were too young. You need some experience and maturity to get the best out of something like that. If you'd waited till you were thirty you'd have made more of it."

Unbidden the thought came into her mind—by thirty she could have given him several children and still been young as an artist. It was too late to think that now.

"Also, you picked the wrong subjects," Valerio went on. "One was featured in the magazine and the others were described. You should have concentrated more on people. Your real gift was always for portraits. It's the life in the human face that you depict so well. Whatever was vibrant and warm and living found a response in you."

He hesitated, but went on after a moment. "That was one of the things that made me love you. You had laughter, but no malice. You had the gift of life. I wonder if you know what an enchanting quality that is to a man like me. I do not have it myself, but I need to live in its warmth. Whenever I was with you, I would feel as though I had come inside out of the cold, and shut the door behind me. When you left, the light went out of my life, and I have lived in a desert place ever since."

There was a note in his voice she had never heard before. He was speaking with gentle, yearning sadness of the joy and the pain that had shaped him, with regret for what he had lost, but without bitterness.

"I never meant to leave you," she said. "I loved you so much. It was only marriage I didn't want."

"And you tried to tell me that, but I wouldn't listen," he said heavily. "I know. In my heart I've known for a long time what a fool I was. At first I rejected you violently because you had rejected me, and I couldn't endure that. But as time passed my anger faded, and there was only the wretchedness of being without you.

"It got worse and worse. I came to regret sending your letter back without reading it." He smiled faintly. "At one time I even contemplated asking my grandmother what you had said."

"You mean you—"

"Of course I knew she opened it. Do you remember my telling you once how she terrified me when she was determined to do something for my own good?"

"Yes. I know now what you mean."

"Adele had wanted to make me see clearly what I'd done, but it was something I had to learn myself. In the end I came to understand you better—and know the truth about my own feelings."

You knew them then, she thought, but what about now? She was beginning to realize that Valerio spoke of his love only in the past tense, but she wasn't sure if he realized it himself. It might mean nothing. In the old days he had loved her for a long time before he spoke of it. But she would be overjoyed if he'd said right out that he still loved her. He'd said other things that might mean the same thing—or might not. He'd said that she was still in his heart. But still she hungered for the three important little words, especially after she'd admitted her own love so frankly.

"You never actually asked your grandmother about my letter then?" she said.

"No. It was too late. And a plan began to form in my mind, about five years after we broke up. I decided that I had to bury my pride and search for you. You will think this very comic perhaps, but I had an elaborate plan for contriving a meeting and pretending that it had happened by chance."

"I don't think it's comic at all," she said passionately. "I think it would have been wonderful. Oh, Valerio, why didn't you?"

He regarded her with eyebrows raised, and for a moment there was a disconcerting touch of the old cynicism that she had seen these past few weeks. "You'd have come with me?"

"Of course I would."

"Even though you were on the verge of marriage to another man?"

"What?"

"I told you, this was five years ago. The piece about you in the magazine said you were engaged. Naturally, I immediately abandoned the idea of coming to find you."

"Oh—" She had leaned toward him, but now she fell back in her seat, feeling like a doll whose stuffing was falling out. She gave a jerky little laugh. "It's strange, but I'd completely forgotten about Gary. So but for him..." She pulled herself together. "If you forgave me all those years ago, why have you been so bitter toward me recently?"

"Can you imagine the effect on me of discovering that you were planning a marriage to another man, after walking out on *our* wedding? And that while I had been pining for you, you had forgotten me? It turned my love to hate all over again. It was as though your desertion had occurred the day before, as though you had rejected me a second time. In my dreams I heard you laughing at me for my foolish fidelity.

"For the first and only time in my life I went out and got very drunk indeed, quite deliberately. It was Judge Corelli who found me, and prevented my doing some damage, either to myself or to someone else."

"Oh, no!" she was horrified. "Did that mean a black mark in your career?"

He smiled. "You wouldn't say that if you knew the stories of the judge's own youth. No, he told me he was relieved to discover that I was capable of behaving in a thoroughly disreputable fashion like everyone else."

Sadness enveloped her as she thought about how closely they had missed each other, how different everything might have been. "It's terrible to find things out too late," she said, "and to think 'if only...' If only I'd known about that studio—".

"Are you finding it useful?"

"It's a wonderful place, like waking up in Aladdin's cave. If you could see the things I've done in it. I've gone through canvases at a terrible rate. As soon as I've recaptured what I want,

I go on to something else. It's all coming back to me, things I thought I'd forgotten...."

She talked for ten minutes without stopping, carried along on a tide of enthusiasm. Her eyes sparkled and her voice was vibrant as she tried to describe the joy of rediscovery. Valerio listened without saying anything, but his eyes were fond, and he smiled at her.

"I can't tell you what it means to me to discover that I'm still an artist," she said. "It's like finding a..."

She stopped, embarrassed by what she had been going to say.

"Go on," Valerio prompted.

"I was going to say that it's like finding a lover still there waiting for me."

He laughed wryly. "Yes, art was always an alternate lover for you, one that I had to fight, and that eventually won you away from me. How strange that it should be I who reunites the two of you. I'm glad now that I kept that studio as it was. It's been waiting for you all this time."

"Your mother told me you were going to give it to me when we came back from our honeymoon. But I wish I'd known about it. I always thought you didn't understand."

"I only thought of it about three weeks before the wedding. Then I had to rush to get it ready in a few days. I did everything myself, right down to the purchase of the last pencil. With so little time left it seemed a good idea to keep it as a surprise." He looked down and played with his knife as he asked the next question. "Are you telling me that if you had known about the studio...it would have made any difference?"

"I don't know," she said thoughtfully. "I've thought about that a great deal recently. I believe the answer is no. I had to get out and battle my own way in the world. I couldn't have settled for the tower in those days. It would have been too sheltered. I couldn't have appreciated it as I do now."

"That's what I thought you would say." Valerio looked at his watch and turned to catch the waiter's attention. For the first time Helena realized that while they talked she had eaten her way through an entire meal, and never noticed. Her heart began to thump. In a few minutes this wonderful evening with

Valerio would be at an end and their coldly formal relationship would be resumed. Until when? How long would this present suspense last? How would it end? And what would happen to her afterward? She'd been carried high on the euphoria of loving, but now hard reality faced her again.

"I don't want to go back to the villa," she said when they were in the street. "We've just found each other again, and I can't bear to lose you so soon."

"We shall not lose each other, my heart. What we have had today can never be taken away from us. But we must be a little apart until I know you are safe."

"Can't we have just this one night?" she pleaded.

But he shook his head firmly. "It's so hard for me to refuse," he said. "Yet I must. Nor must you try to tempt me, in case I yield and do you a great wrong."

She sighed, knowing it was useless to try to persuade him when his mind was made up. He took her hand and led her toward the Ponte Vecchio, and suddenly she remembered another night just like this one, when they had walked hand in hand across the old bridge. It had looked then exactly as it did now, as it had for hundreds of years. It was a place that was never deserted, for amiable eccentrics came there night and day, as well as lovers.

The first time they'd hardly looked at their surroundings. It had been a fine spring night and they had been lost in the wonder of their newly discovered love. There had been nothing to warn them then of their impending tragedy. Helena remembered that night as the time of her most perfect, unspoiled happiness, a time that could never be repeated through all the years of her life. Looking up at Valerio she knew that he was as torn by memory as herself.

At the crown of the bridge they had to pause because a little crowd blocked their way. At its center stood a young man. He wore a threadbare black velvet cloak that might have come from the nineteenth century, and he was declaiming in a theatrical manner that seemed completely at one with the picturesque setting. Helena tried to place the words, and couldn't.

"He's an actor," Valerio said in her ear. "They can always find an audience here. He's reciting from Dante's *Inferno*."

The actor's voice rang out.

> "Nessun maggior dolore,
> Che ricordarsi del tempo felice
> Nella miseria."

The little crowd applauded enthusiastically. Helena stood motionless, silently repeating the words to herself: In sorrow, there is no greater misery than to remember a time of happiness. She knew that this perfect evening was finally over. Valerio touched her face gently. Then he slipped an arm around her shoulders to lead her away. He took her to the car and pointed it out of Florence, toward the villa. This time she made no protest.

Two days later Valerio hurried into the police station at ten o'clock in the morning. Sergeant Torrini looked up. "The chief said to send you in as soon as you arrived," he said. "You know the way."

Chief of Police Manzini looked up with a grunt of satisfaction as Valerio entered his office. He was a man in his fifties with gray-streaked hair, the build of a prizefighter and sharp eyes.

"I'm grateful to you for seeing me at once," said Valerio formally.

"I wanted to see you anyway. I called you yesterday but no one knew where you were."

"I was interviewing a witness." Valerio seated himself and started to take papers from his briefcase. "Signora Catesby's amnesia has started to pass. The day before yesterday she managed to tell me how she came to be driving that night. As I suspected, it was Brian Hanley who had been drinking. He was actually in the driver's seat when they started out.

"Signora Catesby had originally refused to drive on the grounds that she was not in possession of a license. She suggested waiting at Santi's place overnight. It was Lucilla Dorani herself who vetoed that suggestion.

"At the bottom of the slope the car swerved off the road. It was this that persuaded Signora Catesby to take over the driving. I know the place she described and I spent yesterday trying to get some independent confirmation of what she told me."

"And did you get any?" said Manzini.

"A certain amount, yes. I interviewed the occupants of the nearby houses and eventually found one who was a partial witness to the incident. He didn't see much, but he heard a good deal. He was woken in the early hours by the noise and looked out of his bedroom window. He could just make out that a car had gone off the road. I will read you what he says."

Valerio took out a paper and began to quote.

"I could see that a woman had got out of the car and was standing by the driver's window. She appeared to be arguing with a man inside. I only know a little English, but I think she was using that language. The man was laughing all the time. She raised her voice. In the end she opened the door and helped him out. He was still laughing. He got into the back seat, and she took his place. Then she drove off."

Valerio pushed the paper across the desk.

"His name and address are at the bottom," he said. "I've told him that the police will want to talk to him."

"It would help if he'd come forward in the first place," said Manzini irritably. "Why didn't he?"

"Why should he? He had no idea that what he'd seen related to the Dorani case. He saw a man, a woman and a car, none of them well enough to identify individually. If Helena Catesby had told this story earlier he'd have made the connection, but she wasn't able to."

"As you point out, he can't make a positive identification."

"True. But if the car he saw wasn't Brian Hanley's, and if the woman who got out and argued in English wasn't Helena Catesby, that is straining coincidence. As a matter of fact, I can offer some evidence on that point, too. There'd been rainfall the day before the accident, and the soil was soggy enough to show tire marks. But there's been nothing but sun every day since, and the soil dried out like iron, still with the marks in it. Here," Valerio said, tossing a photograph over the desk. "I took my camera with me. You can see the marks quite clearly." He gave Manzini time to study the picture before adding calmly, "Those marks tally perfectly with the tire on Hanley's car—as this picture will show."

He handed another picture to Manzini, who studied both of them with a furrowed brow.

"May I ask," he said at last, "just how you got access to Hanley's car, which is in police custody?"

Valerio smiled.

"And the judge called you a man of honor," Manzini growled.

"I also visited the firm from which Hanley hired that car," Valerio went on. "Luckily they keep meticulous records, covering all details of every vehicle. They will swear that those tires were on that car when Hanley collected it."

"All right, I don't doubt it," said Manzini.

"I've taken the step of placing my evidence in your hands because I believe I'm in a position to ask for the drinking charge to be dropped altogether," said Valerio. "Any independent check you do will only confirm these details. That, plus Hanley's behavior, is surely conclusive. You cannot seriously continue to believe that my client had been drinking when she took the wheel of that car?"

"I don't," Manzini said unexpectedly. "I concede the point. The business about the license has already been dealt with. That leaves only the charge of causing an accident by reckless driving."

"But that—"

"And if I might be allowed to get a word in edgeways," said the police chief, raising his voice and speaking with some exasperation, "playing detective and teaching the police their job is all very well, Lucci. But just occasionally we *do* manage to get the evidence before some smart young lawyer."

Valerio grimaced and fell silent.

"As I told you," Manzini resumed, "I tried to get hold of you yesterday. What you've just told me fills in all the pieces of the jigsaw except one. Well, I have that one."

Valerio stared. "Do you mean that Lucilla Dorani—"

"Signorina Dorani became conscious yesterday morning. What's more, for one hour before she woke she was talking in her sleep."

"You mean she actually remembers everything?"

"Far from it. After the length of time she's been unconscious, that was hardly to be expected. But she remembers one vital thing. She knows what happened in the very last seconds before the smash. They seem to be engraved on her brain, because the poor child can't stop herself going over them. Here." Manzini took out a notebook. "It's slightly irregular, but in the circumstances, you'd better see the notes for yourself. See what she says."

Valerio stared hard at the page for a few minutes, feeling a heaviness take possession of him.

"So that was it," he said at last. "So simple. And none of us thought of it." He pulled himself together and forced himself to speak normally. "Does Ranelli know this?"

"No. He wasn't permitted to see her. Read further down the page and you'll see why. Naturally, he was upset about not being allowed in, and he nearly got himself arrested for assaulting a police officer."

"I can imagine," Valerio said blankly, his eyes still on the page and the few simple words that would separate him from Helena Catesby.

"Do you object if I tell Ranelli?" he went on, speaking with an effort.

"I'd be glad if you would. He's got to know sooner or later, and I'm damned if I'm going to waste time calming him down. If he doesn't learn to control that nasty temper of his, he's going to end up in serious trouble."

The eyes of the two men met across the desk, in perfect mutual comprehension.

"I wonder what he would have done if he'd known this," Valerio said, laying the notes on the desk.

"I don't exactly know what happened in the Straw Market," Manzini said. "I've heard rumors, but not hard facts. No one wants to be witness, probably because they don't want to admit that they stood there and let it happen. So it's up to Signora Catesby to tell her story if she wants to press charges."

"I doubt that she'll do that," Valerio said. "Naturally, it is her decision, but, in the circumstances, I shall advise her against bringing charges against Guido Ranelli."

"That's what I thought," said Manzini.

Eleven

When Valerio arrived at the Heart of Mercy Hospital an hour later, he found Ranelli in the downstairs reception area, pacing the floor with swift, angry steps. He turned and scowled when he saw Valerio.

"I have nothing to say to you. Nor am I interested in anything you may say to me. I suppose I have you to thank that I can't get in to see her."

"That has nothing to do with me," said Valerio coldly. "Nor do I wish to waste more time with you than I have to. But I have something to tell you. Lucilla regained consciousness yesterday and has told the police how the collision occurred. She doesn't remember everything, but she recalls the last few seconds with absolute clarity."

Ranelli stopped in his tracks, a wolfish smile on his face. "So it is finished," he said. "Now at last someone has spoken a truth that even you cannot suppress, and Helena Catesby will be put where she belongs."

Valerio's features remained impassive as he thrust a paper toward Ranelli. "Lucilla's words are undoubtedly the truth," he said. "Read them."

Ranelli snatched the paper and wheeled away. But almost immediately he turned on Valerio.

"Do you think I am such a fool as to believe this?" he shouted.

"Without doubt you are a fool," Valerio said. "A moment ago you claimed that Lucilla could only have spoken the truth. Now you try to claim it is a lie."

"The police made her say this."

The nun on the reception desk was looking up, frowning at the commotion. Valerio reached out an arm and grasped Ranelli hard by the shoulder, thrusting him down onto a nearby seat. He sat beside him and spoke in a sharp, urgent voice. "Shut up," he said, "and try to control yourself! A moment's thought will show you that you are talking nonsense. The police thought they had a case against Helena Catesby. Do you think they wanted Lucilla to demolish it the way she has?

"Besides," he added after a moment, "the police in this city are honorable men. They're not in the habit of putting words into the mouths of witnesses. Manzini isn't pleased, but he immediately accepted the fact that this clears Signora Catesby."

Ranelli stared stupidly down at the paper he was holding in his hand, silently reading Lucilla's words over and over again:

"I was scared. Brian Hanley kept interfering with the driving. I begged him to stop but he was too drunk to listen. He leaned forward from the back seat and grabbed the wheel. When I saw the truck I turned and tried to push him away, but he kept hold of the wheel and he wouldn't let it go. I screamed because he was taking us into the path of the truck—and then it hit us."

"I will kill that man," said Ranelli slowly.

Valerio shrugged. "Do what you like," he said indifferently. "I have no interest in protecting Hanley. But he is a public man. I doubt it will be possible to get him back here, but the publicity will finish his parliamentary career, and probably damage his business severely, too. If you have the patience to wait a little we may all enjoy the pleasure of seeing him ruined.''

Ranelli raised his head. ''And of course, you have yet another vendetta to pursue,'' he said. ''How long before I am arrested for the other day's business?''

''I very much hope that you will not be. Manzini is preparing to drop all charges against Signora Catesby. When the formalities have been completed she will be free to leave Florence. If she was still under suspicion, then make no mistake about it, it would give me great satisfaction to pursue you as far as the law can go. As it is, I shall try to make her drop the matter for her own sake. I want no complications to hinder her departure.''

Ranelli gritted his teeth. ''I shall see her,'' he said, ''and apologize.''

''If you make any attempt to see Helena Catesby,'' Valerio said, with soft, deadly intensity, ''I will make you regret the day you were born.''

Before those hard, implacable eyes Ranelli fell back. He turned his face away from Valerio. ''Why am I not allowed to see Lucilla?'' he said. ''She is my fiancée. I should be with her.''

''She will not allow it,'' Valerio said.

''What do you mean? She wouldn't keep me away.''

''I know only what the police have told me. They say she begged not to have to see you. She is so frail that they have to yield.''

Ranelli stared at him. ''I don't understand. She loves me.''

''But she also fears you. Perhaps now you should consider how much you are to blame for what has happened, Ranelli.''

''*I?* Is it my fault she was at that place?''

''To a certain extent, yes. I warned you once before that you were suffocating that girl. I said that eventually she would rebel, and that rebellion is rarely without cost. You both would have to pay the price, Ranelli, and the blame for it would be yours.''

''I wanted only to protect her. She's so young...''

''Too young, perhaps, for you. She was not ready for you to 'take possession' of her, and in her own way she was trying to show you that. Signora Catesby urged that the journey home should be abandoned, and all three of them should ask Santi to put them up for the night. It was Lucilla who insisted on coming home in the car, despite the fact that she knew Hanley was drunk, because she was desperate to prevent your finding out where she had been. My God, if I thought a woman I loved was so afraid of me that she would risk her life rather than— Well, no matter."

There was no aggression left in Ranelli now. He looked as if he'd received a body blow. The sight stirred Valerio to a moment's pity, and when he spoke again it was in a kinder voice. "I know you love Lucilla more than your own life. It's hard for a man to accept that that is not enough. It may be that such love is not what a woman most needs. It may be that the truest proof of love is to open your hands and let her go free."

Ranelli said nothing. He was staring at the floor. Gradually his head dropped until it was resting on his hands. For a moment Valerio rested a hand lightly on his shoulder. Then he left him.

"*Signora*, you are wanted on the telephone. It is the master."

"Thank you, Nina."

Helena wiped her hands on her smock and ran down two flights of stairs. It was two days since she'd heard Valerio's voice, and already that seemed so terribly long. "Valerio?"

"Make sure you're sitting down. I have some news for you."

"I'm sitting. What's happened?"

"It's over. There are no charges against you."

"Wh—what?"

"Lucilla came round yesterday morning. She remembers enough to clear you. The accident was Hanley's fault. I'll explain in more detail when I see you tonight. I'm coming to dinner, but I thought you'd like to know that you're in the clear.

"There are still some formalities to be gone through. The police want to get a proper statement from Lucilla, and that may take a few days, given the state she's in. Until that's happened, the charges won't be officially dropped. But I saw Chief Manzini this morning and he told me, off the record, that there are no plans to proceed against you on any charge at all. You should be free to go in less than a week."

"Free to go?"

Somewhere in the distance she heard the sound of a buzzer. Valerio's voice came again.

"Someone's just arrived. I can't talk now. I'll see you this evening. Will you inform my mother, please?"

He was gone suddenly, and she was left staring at the phone. The news had come so abruptly that she could hardly take it in. She was cleared. The nightmare was over. And Valerio had informed her in a voice of impersonal cheerfulness that she was free to go.

But of course, she realized, he was in his office. His secretary was probably in the room with him. Valerio was the last man to speak of personal things under these circumstances. So she tried to reassure herself, but still there was a dark fearful place in her heart.

She heard a noise from the doorway and looked up to find Maria watching her. "I was just coming to find you," Helena said. "That was Valerio. He's coming to dinner tonight. He's managed to get all the charges against me dropped. Lucilla is conscious again and...I'm cleared."

Maria closed her eyes. "Thank God!" she breathed. "Then you will soon be leaving us *signora*?"

"Yes, I suppose I will."

"There can be nothing to keep you, now my son's duty toward you is done." Maria came farther into the room. "I do not like you *signora*, but I believe you have some sense of decency—too much to want to damage my son. You owe him so much. You will not repay it by harming him again, I know."

"Harming him?"

Maria gave her chilly smile. "By trying to trap him in a resumption of your old relationship. By trying to force him into marriage. But I'm sure that you realize that's out of the question. He's a lawyer. He can't be married to a woman who has been connected with scandal.''

''But I'm cleared, I'm innocent...''

''Yes, but you were charged, and people remember these things. Moreover, it is only because of my son's adroitness that you haven't spent these past few weeks in prison.

''You went to a party at the house of Lorenzo Santi, a man of foul reputation. I accept that you acted in ignorance, but the world will not believe it. Finally, you are divorced. That is still a very serious matter in this country.''

''Are you trying to say that marriage to me would ruin Valerio?''

''Let us say that it would do him no good. For a lawyer, who must maintain an impeccable reputation, marriage to a woman in your...circumstances would not be advisable.''

''That's for Valerio to say,'' said Helena angrily.

''Of course. I have never tried to dictate my son's actions since he became a man. Otherwise I should have advised him not to try to make you his wife ten years ago. You were plainly unsuitable even then, although I tried to make the best of you. I wasn't surprised when you behaved badly. Now I give you the credit of expecting you to behave well, and not repay his generosity by doing what would harm him.

''Not, to be frank, that I think you will get the chance. Valerio will not be a fool twice. He is as aware as I am of how dangerous you are to his reputation, to all he has worked so hard to build up. He is aware of his obligations to his family. I think he will not attempt to introduce a woman like yourself into our midst.''

She began to walk away. At the door she turned for a brief moment. ''Did Valerio mention any particular time?'' she inquired in her gracious, silvery voice.

''He said nothing about time.''

''Then he will be here at the normal time. I expect.'' Maria floated away.

Helena stared after her, sick at heart. It was easy to tell herself that Maria was trying to frighten her off, that she believed what she wanted to believe. It was less easy to silence the inner voice that reminded her of how determinedly Valerio had resisted looking beyond this point, or allowing her to look.

He had said, "We don't know what the future holds," and she'd thought he was referring to the charges hanging over her. But might he not have been talking about his own inner confusion about what he wanted from her?

But perhaps he wasn't confused. Perhaps he'd always intended to send her away when the case had concluded satisfactorily. She remembered how insistent he had been that their relationship should return to being a distant professional one. Had it been for her sake, or had he been anxious to avoid a scandal for himself?

It might be possible to dismiss Maria's assertion that Valerio was "aware of his obligations to his family" as the wishful thinking of a woman clinging to the standards of another age. But it wasn't possible to dismiss the memory of Valerio's own voice saying "with us the family is all important," when he had first explained to her the sacrifice of his own ambitions to please his father. What would he sacrifice to please his mother?

Or would it perhaps be no sacrifice at all? He hadn't told Helena directly that he still loved her. She'd believed that he did, convinced that what had happened between them had forged a loving bond that could never be broken again. But suppose he had simply taken what she offered as reparation for an old injury, content afterward to send her on her way, honor satisfied?

Most ominous of all was the memory of Valerio saying, "I am a lawyer. I do not wish it said that I was once engaged to a woman who is now serving a prison sentence."

Of course Valerio was keenly aware of his reputation. How could it be otherwise? Helena had no intention of meekly accepting Maria's structures. The decision was Valerio's. But in her heart she knew she had taken the first tiny step toward accepting the possibility of rejection.

That evening she waited for him in the usual place. She knew that Adele would tell him where she was, and she couldn't bear to have to wait till the end of the evening for a private talk. She was wearing the chiffon dress, and around her shoulders was the white silk scarf she had worn once before. She'd found it in the same spot the next morning, where Valerio had left it.

She heard his steps on the path and whirled to see him. As soon as she saw him all the worries went out of her head. She'd be unhappy later. For now she would simply enjoy having him near. So she opened her arms and he came into them at once.

When he had held her tightly for a long moment he drew back and spoke exultantly, "I promised you, didn't I, that I would keep you safe?"

"Is it really over?"

"All except the shouting. Lucilla's a little more alert today, and she has confirmed her story. Hanley took you into the path of that truck. He leaned over from the back and yanked at the wheel."

She frowned. "I don't remember that. But I do remember the wheel seeming to come alive in my hand, and turning as if of its own accord."

"That was his doing. You may never remember it. You probably didn't even realize at the time what had caused the swerve, but Lucilla is definite. She was turning around, trying to make him let go."

"Is she going to be all right?"

"Eventually, yes. She should make a complete recovery, but it'll take time. However, that may be a blessing in disguise, as it will force a postponement of her marriage. They both need time to think."

He kissed her, but only briefly, before leading her back to the bench, and sitting beside her.

"Tell me the rest," she begged. "What about the things I did remember?"

"The police accept completely that you weren't drunk. Luckily I found some evidence to back up our story...."

He related what he had done concerning the witness and the tire marks. She stared at him. "You did all that? Then it wasn't just Lucilla's memories that got me off. It was you."

"I told you I would!"

He was radiant with triumph. She looked at him with a lump in her throat. This mature, confident man suddenly seemed more endearingly boyish than she could ever remember seeing him. She longed to know if his happiness came from protecting her, or from a successful conclusion to a case. But whichever it was, he was entitled to his moment.

"Yes, you told me," she said, kissing him again. "And now that you've done it, I don't know what to say. But for you, I'd be in prison this minute. There's no way I can ever repay you for what you've done."

"Never mind that," he said hastily. He removed her arms and went to stand at the edge of the arbor, looking out over Florence. "In any case," he said, "the British consulate is paying my bill, so there's no need for you to think of the matter again."

He had his back to her, so he did not see the openmouthed way she stared at him. While she was struggling to find her voice he went on, "There's something else I want to talk about. I went to the hospital and saw Guido Ranelli. He accepts that he was wrong about you. He even spoke of coming to apologize, but I told him if he tried to see you I'd make him sorry he was born."

"Thank you. I don't really want to see him again, even for an apology."

"The question is, what are you going to do about him? The police can only prosecute with your testimony. I told Chief Manzini I'd try to persuade you against a prosecution."

"All right. But why?"

"Because in a few days you'll be free to leave, and I don't want any complications. I don't want anything dragging you back here, or reminding you of what's happened. If you were still under suspicion you'd have nothing to lose by a prosecution. As it is, I want to put an end to the whole business as quickly as possible.''

Her heart sank lower with every word he spoke. It was true, then. Valerio planned to be rid of her, and to achieve this he wanted to cut their professional as well as their personal ties.

But she looked at him with her head up. She wouldn't blame him. After what he had done for her, he was entitled to consider his own welfare.

"I'll do whatever you advise," she said.

"There's something more. This is difficult to say, and I don't know if I can make you understand..."

"I do understand," she said quickly. "You don't need to explain. You want me to go away, don't you?"

"Yes, for a while. I want you to go back to England, and see me from a distance." He smiled in wry self-mockery. "You'll find that a few hundred miles cuts me down to size."

"Valerio, please don't talk like this. You don't have to. I'm in love with you. In a sense I've been in love with you for the past ten years. But that's my problem. If you don't want me, then you don't. I'll learn to live with it. But I'm not seventeen anymore. Don't start telling me I'll 'grow out of you' because I won't."

"I should have told you that when you *were* seventeen," he said roughly.

"No! It wasn't true!"

He turned swiftly toward her. His eyes were haggared. "It might be true now, though. I told you once that you were intoxicated with danger. People who live through danger together often do fall in love, do you know that? But what about afterward, when the danger is past? I want you to find out what you feel about me when you're *not* dependent on me, not while I'm still wearing the shining armor.

"If I had any doubts that I'm doing the right thing, you set them to rest a moment ago when you talked about being unable to repay me. That's the last thing I want you to be thinking and feeling. I took advantage of you once, Helena. I'm not going to do it again."

"If you loved me," she said with a touch of belligerence, "you *would* 'take advantage' of me."

"Be as selfish as I was ten years ago, you mean? Rush you off your feet while you're in too much of a haze to know what you're feeling? Not again!

"As for my not wanting you, let me tell you something. When Manzini showed me Lucilla's words and I saw that they cleared you, do you know what my first reaction was? *My heart sank.* You were safe, and all I could think of was that now I'd have to let you go. God forgive me, I actually wanted to keep you here, helpless and dependent on me. A man enjoys slaying the dragon and laying it at the lady's feet. I'm sorry if that sounds chauvinistic, but there it is. I'm not proud of it."

"As a matter of fact," she said crossly, "you don't remind me a bit of St. George. You did once, but now you look more like Don Quixote, being idiotically chivalrous and getting everything wrong! You might credit me with enough intelligence to know my own mind."

"Yes well, my experience of you has been that you do sometimes change your mind," he said with quiet irony. "I'm sorry, Helena, I didn't mean to drag up the past again, and I'm not casting it at you in anger this time. But try to understand that I have my own reasons for wanting you to be quite sure."

"And what will convince you that I'm 'quite sure'?"

"Go back to England. Get some miles between us, and some time. If you're still in love with me in three months—"

"Three months?"

"Then send for me and I'll come to you. We'll talk then."

"Valerio, if you love me, don't do this. I understand that you're afraid, but don't do it. If you send me away now we'll never come together again, I know it!"

"We will if you want us to."

"No!" she said desperately. All her instincts were telling her that this was a terrible mistake. "You're trying to do what you think you should have done ten years ago. But you can't put the clock back that way. What would have been right then is wrong now. If you're afraid I'll walk out again, we'll go to the near-

est town hall and fix the wedding for the first possible date. Tomorrow if you like."

"No, thank you," he said with a touch of chill. "What would that achieve? If you changed your mind after our marriage you'd still leave me. Have you forgotten that you said as much only a short time ago in this very spot?"

"But I was talking about something quite different."

"You were talking about being smothered by my possessiveness. Well, I haven't changed. I'm still a possessive man."

"You can be as possessive as you like, it can't harm me now. Ten years ago I was scared you'd swallow me up because I was too green and ignorant to stand up for myself. But I'm strong enough to do that now. I'm not afraid of you anymore. But I'm terribly afraid of losing you."

She knew at once that she'd said the wrong thing. He put his hands on her shoulders and stared very seriously into her face.

"That's exactly what I mean. All this time you've had nothing but my hand to hold on to. Now the time has come to let it go, you're afraid. But that isn't love. Maybe you love me as well, but you need time to find out. And I'm going to make you take that time."

"I didn't mean 'afraid' in that sense," she pleaded, frantic to make him understand. "I meant that I love you with all my heart, and to lose you again would be the worst thing that could happen to me. Oh, why can't you understand something that's so simple and obvious?"

"Because for me it's not simple and obvious." Valerio passed a hand over his eyes. "Please, darling, try to understand. I'm doing what I believe is right. Don't make it harder. I hope that in time we'll be together. But I've seen too many female clients imagine they're in love with the lawyer while the case is on, and forget his face the following week."

"And how often does the lawyer become infatuated with the client because he has enjoyed playing St. George?" said Helena in a hard voice, to cover the pit of fear that was opening inside her.

He sighed. "That happens sometimes too. The difference is that the client briefly imagines that it's forever, and the lawyer always knows differently. So he's the one that has to be sensible."

"Damn being sensible! I'm in love with you. If you're not in love with me, have the courage to say so."

He looked at her bleakly. "I honestly don't know how to answer that, Helena. I'm just asking you for a little time—mainly for you, but for me too, perhaps."

She felt as though all the breath had gone out of her. This was what Maria had told her would happen. Valerio was distancing himself for her. He was doing it gently and in a way that would save her face, but the message was unmistakable. He was trying to tell her that the kindest thing she could do for him was to go away and cause him no more harm. If, in three months' time, she was so foolish as to contact him, he would simply never be available. But he trusted her not to be that foolish.

"If that's the way it is," she said, keeping her voice steady, "then of course I have no more to say. Shall we go in now? They must be waiting for us."

Four days later Helena was packing her things for departure. There was only a little more to do. In an hour Giorgio would be calling for her with the car. He would take her to the station, where she would catch the train for Pisa, which had the closest airport to Florence.

She was now formally free of all charges. Her passport had been returned to her the evening before. Valerio had brought it himself when he came to dine at the villa. He was courteous, pleasant, even charming. But there was nothing in his manner that reached out to her, and when he had politely offered to accompany her to the station in the morning she had equally politely told him not to trouble himself.

Now she wanted only to get away—away from Maria with her smile of catlike satisfaction; away from Adele with her rambunctious warmhearted matchmaking; away from Valerio with his remoteness. Above all she wanted to escape forever from Florence, which had become a place of bittersweet memories for the second time in her life.

When the suitcase was ready Giorgio came to take it downstairs for her. She was standing in the drive, watching him load it into the trunk of the car when she saw a taxi drive up to the gates of the villa, John Driffield of the British consulate got out.

"Glad to see you looking so well after all that's happened," he said, advancing toward her with his hand outstretched.

She greeted him warmly. To him, too, she owed a debt of gratitude.

"Just off, are you?" he said. "That's right. Nice to see it all turned out so well. Thought I'd come and say goodbye properly. I meant to bring your passport. In fact, I went to the police station for it, but your lawyer was there before me and he insisted on taking it. Got the feeling he didn't like me much."

"Didn't like you? Why on earth shouldn't he?"

"Can't think. Never met the fellow before this, although I've heard of his reputation, of course. Everyone has. But it was obvious that he didn't want me here. I began to wonder why."

"I expect you imagined it," said Helena. "What possible reason could there be?"

Driffield cast a look at Giorgio, then said to Helena, "Mind if we walk on a bit? I'd like to talk in private."

"I don't think Giorgio speaks English, but all right."

They strolled away down one of the paths and Helena led him to a sheltered bench.

"I'm probably making a mountain out of a molehill," Driffield said. "After all, the fellow's done a damn fine job for you, but..."

"But what?"

"It occurred to me that the reason he didn't want me calling here might be because he didn't want you to say too much to me. So I thought I'd make a point of calling anyway, just to say goodbye. You don't have anything to say about him, do you? Any...shall we say, complaints?"

So Valerio really was determined to protect himself from her at all costs. By now she was almost inured to that pain and she managed to answer promptly, "Not a thing. I can assure you that Signor Lucci has never for one moment taken advantage of the fact that I'm living in his house, or abused his position of trust in any way."

Driffield visibly relaxed. "That's all right then. It's just that with his having known you personally, and taking the case in such an unusual way—"

"Wait a minute," Helena interrupted him. "What do you mean, unusual?"

"Well, it was very unusual. He virtually beat down the consulate door demanding to be assigned to your case. Otherwise you'd never have got him. A man of Lucci's magnitude doesn't normally touch this kind of thing. Not big enough for him. In fact I was on the verge of telephoning another lawyer for you when I got a call from someone very high up indeed to say that the case was to go to Advocate Lucci."

"How high up?"

"Higher up that I'm prepared to be specific about. But Lucci had been pulling strings, I can tell you. Said he was an old friend of yours and wanted to help you out. When he offered to do it for nothing, of course officialdom fell all over him."

"For nothing?"

Driffield studied her, alarmed. "Are you telling me you didn't know all this? I naturally assumed—I mean, he *is* an old friend, or was he making that up?"

"No, he wasn't making it up. We did know each other once before but..." She recovered herself hastily, realizing that she had to be careful of what she said. "When I first talked to him I hadn't been conscious for very long, and my mind was still vague. I expect I got a lot of things wrong. I formed the impression that it was pure coincidence that he was my lawyer. You see, he never knew me under my married name, so I naturally thought...in fact I don't see how he knew it was I."

"I can't help you there, but there was something in the papers the day after it happened. Maybe he saw that. You were still unconscious at the time. Funny he never told you though, isn't it? But as you say, you were hazy. I expect he did tell you, and you forgot. Anyway, it makes no difference now, does it?''

"Of course not," Helena said. "How could it? I'm very grateful to you, Mr. Driffield, for taking the trouble to come to see me. You'll never know how grateful."

It was barely five minutes later that John Driffield departed, but to Helena, longing for him to go and leave her with her thoughts, it seemed an age. When at last the villa gates had clanged behind him, she whirled and confronted Giorgio.

"I want to go to Signor Lucci's office," she said. "Quickly."

"But Signora, the train."

"Don't worry, I'll catch the train. What I want to say won't take long—but it has to be said."

Twelve

———

Valerio's secretary looked up in surprise at Helena's stormy entrance. She hadn't been there on Helena's previous visit, and did not recognize her.

"Is anyone with Signor Lucci?" said Helena.

"No, *signora*, but a client is expected at any moment, and if you don't have an appointment..."

"Don't worry," said Helena. "He'll be free in a few moments." She marched straight into Valerio's office.

He was standing by the window looking out broodingly into the street beneath. But he turned at her entrance, and looked startled.

"Helena, shouldn't you be on your way to catch the train?"

"I had to talk to you first. I've just had a visit from John Driffield of the British consulate." She said the last words slowly and emphatically, and saw him pale. The curse he muttered was more violent than any she had ever heard him use.

"He came because he was worried," she went on. "You were so determined to stop him visiting me that it aroused his suspicions. He wanted to know if I had any 'complaints' about your behavior. I told him I hadn't.''

She paused and met his eyes. But he made no response, just stood looking at her, tension written in every line of him.

''But I have,'' she went on in a quiet voice. ''I have one complaint to make, Valerio. You haven't been honest with me, not from the very first day. You allowed me to believe that it was just coincidence that you were my lawyer. But it wasn't, was it?''

''No,'' he said heavily.

''You knew who I was before you came to the hospital? You knew all the time?''

''Yes, I knew.'' Valerio reached down and opened a drawer in his desk. From it he pulled a paper and handed it to her. ''You might as well see this now.''

It was a newspaper cutting, dated the day following the accident. The picture had evidently been taken immediately after the crash. The photographer had managed to get close to the car on the driver's side. His shot showed Helena, unconscious, her head flung back, her face clearly visible. Also visible was the silver filigree pendant around her throat.

''So that was where you'd seen it,'' she said, amazed.

''Yes, I gave myself away rather clumsily when I mentioned that pendant,'' said Valerio. ''You pounced on my slip with disconcerting speed and I only just managed to talk myself out of it. I made another mistake when we were dining at that restaurant near the Ponte Vecchio when I mentioned that I'd read of your engagement. I was terrified in case you remembered that the magazine had, in fact, mentioned Gary Catesby's name.

''I knew you as soon as I saw that picture. The years haven't changed you so much that I couldn't recognize you. From the details given in the story I realized you were in serious trouble. I had to get you out of it, I didn't ask myself why. I just knew that the thought of you in prison was intolerable to me. It was like a physical pain, and I couldn't endure it.''

Helena had seated herself. She was still staring at the picture. "Mr. Driffield said you practically beat down the doors of the consulate, demanding to be given my case," she said.

"Something like that. I knew you needed the very best man to get you out. When I thought of some of the idiots who might have been assigned to you I went half-crazy. It had to be me. I'm sorry if that sounds conceited."

"No," she said, still bemused. "Mr. Driffield spoke of your reputation, and said you didn't normally take this kind of case because it was too small for you. Besides, no one else would have taken the trouble for me that you have."

"I meant it to be impersonal, I swear I did. For one thing, I thought you were still married. That's why I started off by claiming that it was coincidence. I was afraid your husband might be around and if he knew what lengths I'd gone to to get the case he might get rid of me.

"But I knew as soon as I saw you that it wasn't going to be that easy. When I walked into your room, you were sobbing your heart out. I'd never known you to cry before, except once. You cried on our wedding day, when you were banging on my door, pleading to be let in. The sound had never left me all these years. Hearing it again almost made me throw caution aside and take you in my arms, but by the time you looked up I had collected myself.

"You told me in that first meeting that you weren't married anymore, but you also left me with the distinct impression that you were in love with Hanley. So I had to let you go on believing that we'd met by accident. It hurt my pride that while you'd forgotten me, I'd come running after you."

"But I made it clear to you long ago that I wasn't in love with Brian. You could have told me any time."

"Could I? It's not as easy as you think. Once you've started a deception it gains a life of its own. It's always simpler to just let the matter drop. Besides, I was terrified of what the truth would reveal to you. I was torn in two directions myself. I wasn't indifferent to you. I would have torn the prison down rather than allow you to be carted off there. But the old bitterness and pain were still inside me.

"If you had ever reached out to me in those early days, I think I could have told you. Once I thought it was about to happen. We were in the garden, and there was a moment when it seemed to me that you were about to touch me. If you had done so, I think I would have fallen at your feet."

"I wanted to so much, but I thought you'd despise me. And then over dinner you were so cold and impersonal...."

"I very nearly wasn't at that dinner at all. When I left you I headed for the gates. I wanted to get as far away from you as possible."

"I came out later that night, and found you sitting in the garden with my scarf."

He drew in his breath sharply. "So you *were* there! I felt your presence so close to me, I could almost touch you. But when I looked up, there was no one, and I thought I'd imagined it. I've imagined you with me so often."

"I slipped away before you saw me. I knew you hadn't meant me to see you like that. I was afraid you'd be angry. But all the time I wanted to take you in my arms and tell you how much I still loved you. What would have happened if I had?"

"I think you know the answer. I could not have resisted you any longer. I would have opened my heart to you and we would have been united there and then."

"I wonder," she said longingly, "what your heart would have said to me."

"It would have spoken of its love that was unchanged after so many years and so much suffering. Can you doubt it? Haven't I shown you again and again that you're the only woman I can ever love?"

"And yet you sent me away," she said. "You weren't honest about that, Valerio. You should have told me that I was damaging you. I'd have gone without an argument. I could have borne it more easily if I'd known that you still loved me."

"Damaging me? What on earth are you talking about?"

"I mean you can't marry me because of the scandal. It's strange that I never thought of it before but—"

"Wait a minute!" Valerio took hold of her shoulders and searched her face keenly. "Has my mother been talking to you?"

"A little. But you said yourself that you were thinking of your own reputation. You said you didn't want it known that you were once engaged to a woman who was in prison."

"Rubbish! I had to find a practical reason that you'd accept. That was the best I could think of. Anyway, you haven't been in prison. You're innocent, and now everyone knows it."

"But your mother's right. With everything that's happened, and my divorce—"

"Damn your divorce! What is this nonsense? Do you imagine that my reputation rests on such a shaky basis that such a thing could damage it? Does my mother think so? The two of you have a poor opinion of my abilities then.

"Perhaps for my mother there is some excuse. She grew up in another age, and the old standards still cling to her. But you're a modern woman, Helena. You should know better." He gave a bark of laughter. "So that was why my mother was talking so significantly last night."

"Last night?"

"When I came to the villa for dinner. She and I spoke privately for a few minutes before I left. She referred to your departure obliquely and congratulated me on my good sense. She said she was glad I'd remembered the needs of my family in time. I try never to be less than courteous to my mother, but if I could have spoken freely I'd have said that my family must shift for itself. I sacrificed my ambitions for them, but I won't sacrifice my love.

"Helena, I had no idea that she'd talked to you as well. How could you be so foolish as to listen?"

"Because when we talked the other day, you said you weren't sure of your own feelings, that *you* wanted time to think as well as me."

"You were making it hard for me, darling. I knew that was the one argument that would move you. You kept talking about repaying me until I wanted to bang my head against the wall.

The last thing I want is for you to feel that you owe me anything."

"But you told me a lie," she said indignantly. "You said the British consulate is paying my bill, but John Driffield told me you're not charging them."

"I didn't want to lie to you. I was trying to shift your sense of obligation, because it is the thing that comes between us. I want you to feel absolutely free of me, because true love can only exist between equals. That was why I moved heaven and earth to stop Driffield coming to see you. I knew he'd probably give away my secret. And as soon as you knew I'd defended you for nothing you'd be crushed by a new burden of gratitude, and there'd be more barriers between us."

"Oh, you idiot," she breathed. "Adele was right. The more brilliant a man is the more of a fool he can act."

"Helena, please try to understand! *I do not want you to marry me to settle my bill!*"

"Do you really want me to marry you at all, Valerio?"

"It is what I want with my whole heart and soul. I've never wanted anything so much in my entire life. I want it more now than I did ten years ago, because then I had not discovered the wretchedness of trying to live without you."

"Well then—"

"But I want it for life. I want to know that when you come to my arms you will stay there forever. I don't want to live every day with the fear that you will discover your mistake and leave me desolate a second time. Please, my heart, don't let us have this argument again. I only want you to go home and think. If you want me in three months, I'll still be there, waiting for you."

"But I won't!"

"What?" He stared at her.

"I said I won't still be there in three months. You're making a terrible mistake, Valerio, and it's going to destroy both of us. People do sometimes get two chances in life. You and I are proof of it. *But they don't get three!*

"If you throw away the chance we've been given now, we'll have lost each other forever. I don't know exactly what will happen, but I do know that your nice neat little scenario of meeting again in three months with nothing changed just isn't going to work. Life isn't like that, Advocate Lucci! It isn't neat and tidy, like a legal paper. It's awkward and unpredictable, like a great painting, with all the details the wrong size and shape but everything working together in spite of it.

"You have to take what you're given when you're given it. And if you throw it away, you've no one but yourself to blame if it's lost. That's why I'm telling you that it's now or never. I refuse to go home and twiddle my thumbs, examining my heart under a microscope every day to see if I can notice any changes. I know my own heart *now*. And if you don't know yours yet, then we're wasting our time talking."

"Helena..."

"Either you want me or you don't, Valerio. But this is it! If I go, I go. I'll marry you tomorrow. But I won't marry you in three months."

"I don't like being given an ultimatum."

"That's your misfortune, because I'm giving you one."

"I cannot accept it," he said desperately. "I *will* not accept it. Try to understand, my darling."

"I wonder if I'm beginning to understand more than you think," she said, looking at him keenly.

His eyes were wretched but they hadn't lost their implacable look. "I won't keep you now," he said, "when you're not in a state to make a decision. But I won't give you up easily. If you don't come to me in three months, then I'll come to you."

"You'll be wasting your time. If I leave now I shall sell my flat and use the proceeds to go on another long trip. You've given me back to myself as an artist and I'm going to make the most of it."

"You must do what is right for yourself, Helena. That is all I want you to do."

"Valerio, will you marry me now, or won't you?"

"I will not."

She let out a long, painful breath. "In that case, there's no more to be said. I'll say goodbye now. We won't see each other again. But I have one thing to say before I go. You told me once you weren't out to get revenge. Well, I wonder, because you've enacted the perfect revenge, whether you meant to or not. Last time we broke up I managed to make a life for myself without you—in a sort of way. But I won't get over you this time. You'll be with me to the end of my days as the most wonderful man I ever knew—and the man I lost.

"Do you know what you've done to me, Valerio? Repaying bad with bad is commonplace. But repaying bad with good leaves your victim no recourse.

"I injured you ten years ago, and instead of injuring me back you turned the other cheek, and I can't forgive you for it. Well, let me tell you, your revenge is complete. Because of the generous, forgiving, wonderful way you've acted toward me these past few weeks, I'll love you to the last moment of my life. I'll measure all men against you and reject them all, because they're not you. I'll never have children because you're the only man I could ever want to be their father. I'll live all my life without love, because if I can't have yours I'd rather do without. And that's what you'll have done to me because you lacked a little courage."

"Courage?"

"Yes. And that's the one thing that might reconcile me to your loss. I don't mind that you told me a few white lies, Valerio. I understand about that. I don't even mind that you've been a fraud all this time. Most men are frauds. But what I can't endure is that you're a coward. Because if you weren't, you'd be brave enough to take a few risks for our love. No love worth having ever came without risks. If you can't make yourself take them, I'm finished with you.

"I'm cleared of all charges and I've got my ticket home. You once told me that you wanted me to be strong and free enough to tell you to go to hell. Well, now I'm strong and free, and that's exactly what I'm telling you to do!"

Without waiting for a reply she turned and wrenched open the door. She was through the outer office before anyone could stop her, with only the briefest pause to say to the secretary, "You can tell the client to go in now."

Anger, Helena discovered, was like a drug. The intoxication of it could carry you high just long enough for you to commit yourself to some irrevocable action. Then it could evaporate with dismaying suddenness.

Hers lasted until the train had almost completed its hour-long journey to Pisa. Then she was left with a feeling of weariness and letdown.

At the same time, she wasn't sorry. There had been a deep satisfaction in speaking her mind while the golden-tongued Advocate Lucci listened in stunned silence. And she knew she'd said things that needed saying. Her ultimatum had been no bluff, and Valerio knew her well enough to realize that. Yet he still hadn't budged. He couldn't have told her more plainly that they had no future together. It was better to face that now than to drag out the agony for another three months.

She told herself that she would defer the heartache until she was back in England where she'd have all the time in the world to be miserable. But the heartache refused to be deferred. It was there now, reminding her of what she had lost for the second time, and how much more bitter this final parting would be.

She tried to concentrate on her plans for the future, on the new horizons that beckoned her. But it was impossible to look forward when her heart obstinately looked back at the man she loved and would never see again.

She became aware that the train had stopped some time ago at a tiny station that looked as if it was run by one man and a dog. A very fat man in Helena's compartment was looking out the window and making impatient noises.

"The signal's still against us," he said crossly. "I don't know what's the matter. Normally this train doesn't stop here at all." He had looked back to address the other passengers, but now a noise from outside the window drew his attention and he put his head out again. After a moment he drew back, full of excitement. "We've been stopped by the police. They must be after someone."

Helena felt a stab of alarm. It was ridiculous, of course, but her recent experience had left her unduly sensitive to any mention of police. She spared a moment's pity for whoever was about to be arrested.

The fat man had left the window and crossed to the door so that he could look out into the corridor. "They're coming to this car," he said with relish. "They've started to go through the compartments."

"Is there any need to enjoy it so obviously?" Helena said in a sharp tone.

"*Signora*, you don't understand. The police are searching for a criminal. It is the interests of us all that he be apprehended. He may be violent. We must hope not. *Scusi!*"

This last exclamation was addressed to someone in the corridor. The fat man backed away to make room for the newcomer, and Helena recognized Sergeant Torrini. In the same instant he looked and noticed her. His face lit up with relief and he pushed past the fat man.

"Here you are at last, *signora*," he said. "I've had to search the entire train for you."

There was total silence as all eyes turned toward Helena. She felt panic begin to grip her. "But why? I'm cleared. All the charges against me were dropped."

"There are still formalities to be gone through. I'm afraid you must come with me."

"I will not! I was told I could leave the country and that's what I'm going to—"

Then she saw Valerio standing in the compartment door. He was smiling.

"Thank you, Sergeant, you may now leave this to me," he said smoothly. He inclined his head toward the other passengers. "Forgive the inconvenience, *signori*, but the matter was urgent. Now that we have found the person we were looking for, the train may proceed without further delay."

Even through her indignation Helena recognized the persona that Valerio was projecting. This was his courtroom self, the one that did not shrink from melodrama. He was playing his role this minute as to the manner born.

"Is this woman a criminal?" the fat man demanded.

"A hardened case, I fear," Valerio said sadly. "She tricked her way out of custody this morning and almost managed to get out of the country, but—" his hand shot out and grabbed Helena's wrist "—now I have her safe, and she is returning with me."

"I most certainly am not!" Helena exploded. "I've finished with you once and for all!"

"That is no longer a matter for you to say, *signora*," said the sergeant, entering into the spirit of the thing. "The law must take its course."

"Valerio, let me go at once," she said fuming. "I am not coming with you! Do you understand that?"

But she made the mistake of looking up into his eyes. What she saw there made her heart turn over. They were dancing with an exhilaration she'd never seen before. "I'm not coming with you!" she repeated, since he didn't seem to have taken it in the first time.

"I am afraid that you are," he said. "Look."

She looked down and saw the steel circle about her wrist. There was a matching circle about Valerio's wrist. While she'd been arguing he had handcuffed her to him.

"*How dare you!* You must be quite mad!"

He had drawn her firmly to her feet. Now his eyes looked directly down into hers as he said softly, "On the contrary. I have come to my senses. You are very persuasive, heart of my heart."

"*Three months!*" she reminded him.

"Oh, no. The sentence I have in mind is *much* longer than that."

He began to maneuver her toward the compartment door. Curious glances followed them all the way. At the exit of the train Valerio jumped down first and she hesitated, confronted with the steep steps. She took them gingerly, but after the first two he pulled her gently toward him and in a moment she was on the platform, with his free arm holding her firmly to him. Somehow her own free arm had found its way around his neck for safety.

"How dare you do this to me!" she muttered.

"Forgive me, heart of my heart, but it was the only way to stop the train. Another few minutes and you would have gone. After what you said to me, I was afraid that once you'd left the country I would never get you back. Desperate measures were called for."

"I'd have come back—if you'd really wanted me."

"Perhaps. But I was not prepared to chance it. That was one risk I didn't dare take. But the others we'll take together. This time we'll make it work."

But she still wasn't sure of him. "Is it just because I called you a few names and walked out?"

"A few names? Do you remember what you said to me? It was full of terrible truths. But it was the other things you said that made my heart listen—about your life once we had parted. I saw in it a mirror image of how my own life would be, barren and empty. I am a coward about that. I have not the courage to face the future without you. I've lived too long alone, and now I'm going to keep you with me forever."

"But you'll be afraid that I'll up and leave you."

He shook the handcuffs. "Nonsense, how can you?"

"Do you plan to keep me in shackles for the rest of my life?" she demanded, incensed.

"One way or another, yes. You either wear that—or this."

He withdrew his arm and reached into his pocket. From its depths he produced the diamond ring she'd returned to him ten years earlier.

"Which?" he asked, his eyes fixed on her intently.

"I'll take the ring," she said with dignity, "but only because it's smaller and more comfortable." The last word was choked off as his mouth came down hard on hers.

When her head stopped spinning she became aware of the sound of cheering. Looking round, bewildered, she realized the windows of the train were packed with spectators enjoying themselves hugely.

"Valerio, do you realize that you're making a spectacle of yourself in public? *You?*"

"Yes, I do realize it," he said through gritted teeth, for even now such a display did not come easily to him. "It was necessary, heart of my heart. But make the most of it, because even for you I doubt I shall ever manage it a second time.''

His mouth crushed hers again. The cheers rose to a roar. The sergeant, who'd stayed behind to retrieve Helena's suitcase, jumped down onto the platform. Grinning, he waved the train on. It gathered speed as it passed through the station and people crowded closer to the windows as they slid by, cheering, waving, laughing with delight at the sight that had brightened everyone's day.

Neither of the two on the platform noticed a thing. They were safe in a world where there was only each other; where there would be only each other all their lives.

Silhouette Desire

COMING NEXT MONTH

TEACHER'S PET
Ariel Berk

Cecily was settling into life as a teacher when Nick began to unsettle things. For both, it was a time for their hearts to speak — and their minds to listen.

HOOK, LINE AND SINKER
Elaine Camp

Roxie was a reporter for Sportspeople, but an expert fisherwoman? Never! She has to deceive Sonny to get an interview with him. But when she fell in love with him, she knew she had to tell him the truth. She just couldn't let him be the one that got away.

LOVE BY PROXY
Diana Palmer

Fired for belly dancing in front of her boss, Amanda was then offered a job as a companion to his mother. Worth hadn't ignored her beauty, but he was determined to bid for her on his own terms.

Silhouette Desire

COMING NEXT MONTH

A MUCH NEEDED HOLIDAY
Joan Hohl

When Kate saw a child lost among the shoppers, she vowed to give the parent a piece of her mind. But what began as a contest of wills between Trace and Kate, became a victory of love, giving their hungry hearts a much needed holiday.

MOONLIGHT SERENADE
Laurel Evans

Emma ran a radio station in Connecticut and when Simon invited her to give a speech, she refused. But when he kept returning at weekends, Emma fell in love. Surely such a hotshot would never be content with her...?

HERO AT LARGE
Aimee Martel

Leslie had to convince Ted Logan that her mission to save the reputation of his school was as important as his job to rescue downed pilots. But capturing his heart would be her biggest mission.

Can anyone tame Tamara?

Life is one long party for the outrageous Tamara.

Not for her wedded bliss and domesticity.

Fiercely independent and determined to stay that way, her one goal is to make a success of her acting career.

Then, during a brief holiday with her sister, Tamara's life is turned upside down by Jake DeBlais, man of the world and seducer of women...

Discover love in full bloom in this exciting sequel to Arctic Rose, by Claire Harrison.

Available from May 1986.

Price £2.25.

WORLDWIDE